PETER
DARK

REGINALD Evelyn Peter Southouse Cheyney (1896-1951) was
born in Whitechapel in the East End of London. After serving
as a lieutenant during the First World War, he worked as
a police reporter and freelance investigator until he found
success with his first Lemmy Caution novel. In his lifetime
Cheyney was a prolific and wildly successful author, selling, in
1946 alone, over 1.5 million copies of his books. His work was
also enormously popular in France, and inspired Jean-Luc
Godard's character of the same name in his dystopian sci-fi
film *Alphaville.* The master of British noir, in Lemmy Caution
Peter Cheyney created the blueprint for the tough-talking,
hard-drinking pulp fiction detective.

PETER CHEYNEY

DARK INTERLUDE

DEAN STREET PRESS

Published by Dean Street Press 2022

All Rights Reserved

First published in 1947

Cover by DSP

ISBN 978 1 915014 29 0

www.deanstreetpress.co.uk

To the Maquis

Grateful acknowledgement for technical details in Chapter Four is made to Wing Commander D. Crowley-Milling, DSO, DFC, RAF

CHAPTER ONE
O'MARA

SHAUN Aloysius O'Mara came round the shadow of the low wall that bounded the end of the little church. He stepped unsteadily over the wall; began to walk through the small graveyard towards the yew-tree grove.

It was hot. The sun beat down pitilessly; there was no air. O'Mara stumbled over a low headstone, cursed horribly; saw over his shoulder the short figure of the curé; the dingy worn and shiny *soutane*; the thin white face.

He began to laugh. He laughed at the priest. He began to sing a ribald song in the Breton tongue. The curé shrugged his shoulders; disappeared into the cool darkness of the porch. O'Mara heard his footsteps die away. He thought that the sound of worn shoes on the stone flags was a strange sound.

He was half drunk. He was always at least half drunk. Pints and gallons of spirits, of cheap beer, of *cachaça* of *veritable* cognac that was *veritable* methylated spirit and colouring, had deadened his metabolic processes. Gallons of cheap-cut, laced and doctored wine, had filled his veins with acid, yellowed his eyes, sagged his facial and stomach muscles.

O'Mara was tall and big. Once he had looked like a handsome bull. A well-kept, superior, fierce and handsome bull. Now the skin under his blue eyes was faded and pouchy; the fresh complexion had turned to the greyish hue of the near third-stage drunkard. The fair shining hair that had curled back from an intelligent forehead in waves that made most women envious was long, dank, dirty, bedraggled.

He stepped over the low boundary wall on the far side of the graveyard. There was no shadow here. The sun descended on his bare head without mercy. He could feel it burning through the thick hair on the top of his head, heating the brown and dirty skin of his neck.

He was dressed in a pair of blue velveteen trousers that were baggy at the top and narrow over the broken shoes. He had no socks. As he walked, the trouser legs rode up and you could see his unwashed ankles. He wore a shirt that had been a middle-blue and was now dark blue with dirt and sweat. The shirt was open at the neck; his broad, tanned chest had burst the buttons.

He walked into the yew-tree grove. The damp shadows of the grove; the cool dark box-like square made by the thick arching yew trees, was like an icebox. Outside, it was as hot as hell, he thought. Here, inside the grove, it was as cold as death.

He stumbled over a root, fell; was too tired to get up. He lay there . . . muttering.

He was sorry for himself. The last good eighth of his brain said: This is the third stage—*self-pity,* weakness; sickness; tremors in the left arm and leg; a feeling of approaching paralysis at night; an inability to remember.

O'Mara thought that maybe you could play this game too well. Maybe you could overplay your hand. This drink business was an overrated pastime.

But if the last eighth was still working you were all right; that was what Quayle had said. Quayle had said it would be all right for him because he was O'Mara who could do anything; get away with anything.

He thought: Goddam Quayle. Quayle knew everything. Every goddam thing. Quayle was the boyo for telling you what you could do or what you couldn't do.

O'Mara lay on the damp earth cursing Quayle; mouthing appalling epithets; unspeakable comparisons.

Sometimes you forgot things. *That* was marvellous. It was going to be marvellous for him if he forgot where he'd hidden the coramine and the heroin and the syringe case. That was going to be *very* good.

He began to recite poetry. If you could remember poetry, you were all right. That meant that your brain was still working—more or less. Then he made up his mind to think about himself logically. He was O'Mara—although that was a fact that he divulged only to himself. He was Shaun Aloysius O'Mara who had been born and reared in County Clare. And he could play the piano and ride a horse. He was a good shot; could sail a boat. He spoke four languages. That was who he was and that was what he had been like.

Now he was Philippe Garenne. Not-so-good Philippe. A dirty, drunken sot who worked for Volanon at the *Garage Volanon* on the other side of the estuary. In a minute he would get up and go out of the yew-tree grove and walk to the hill and look over the sunlit estuary. And there on the other side would be the fisherman's cottages and the pseudo hotel that was empty, and the cinema that the Germans had gutted. And on the right, near the quay, where the boats were moored, would be the *Garage Volanon* and the *Café Volanon* just beside it. And the louse Volanon would be standing at the door of the café smoking his curved pipe filled with rank *Caporal,* wondering where the no-good drunken Philippe was. . . . Goddam Volanon . . . to hell with the *Café Volanon* . . . to eternal damnation with the *Garage Volanon*!

He got up. Slowly he got up. He stood there in the cool grove, thinking about the nervous pain in his left arm.

The pain would go in a little while. Of course it would come back. It would be back to-morrow . . . it always came back to-morrow.

He began to think about Eulalia. Now his face changed a little. It became softer. The Senhorita Eulalia Guimaraes . . .*some* Senhorita. The delightful and lovely and alluring Senhorita Eulalia Guimaraes who lived in a delightful and lovely apartment in the Edificio Ultramar, at Copacabana, Rio de Janeiro. His mind swam into a picture that had passed . . . that seemed to have existed such a long time ago.

He saw himself. He was coming out of the bathroom and the sun poured through the open windows of the drawing-room and shone on the off-white carpet; on the primrose-painted walls. He was dressed in a striped dressing-gown—broad stripes of cigar-ash grey and black crêpe-de-chine. *Definitely* a dressing-gown. He wore nothing beneath the robe and he walked across the off-white carpet on his bare feet. Good well-shaped feet that gripped at the carpet like a cat's paws. He walked across the carpet to the radio-gram and put on a record. The soft music of the tango seemed heated with the sunshine.

He stood in front of the radiogram nodding his head to the music; smoking a small black cigar whose perfume he could still smell. . . .

And when he turned round, Eulalia stood in the doorway of the little hall that led from her room. She was dressed in a lacy wrap and he could see the tiny velvet mules beneath. Her hair was dark and her face pale and long, and her lips were cherry colour and her eyes were long and lovely and brown. When she smiled the sun became brighter and the smile curved her mouth and you felt that you wanted to do something about it at once. That you must.

She put her hand against the wall and smiled at him. She said: "It has been said that one can be too happy. This happiness is too sweet to be permanent, my Shaun. Almost . . ."

She went away. He laughed because she was talking nonsense. Sweet nonsense.

He stood there in front of the radiogram listening to the strains of the hot sweet tango, moving his shoulders and his feet in time with the music.

And the bell rang.

And the sound of the door-bell ringing was like coming into the yew-tree grove of which he was then unaware. It was as if someone had laid a dead cold hand on your bare chest. That was how the sound of the door-bell seemed to him.

He went quickly to the door and opened it. Outside, Willis— the English messenger from the Embassy—stood smiling, with the note in his hand.

O'Mara could hear Eulalia saying . . . "This happiness is too sweet to be permanent, my Shaun. Almost . . ."

He took the note, and Willis went away. He opened the note. It was the transcript of a coded message, probably sent in the diplomatic bag by Quayle. It said laconically: *'Come back stop Immediately stop Playtime is over stop Quayle.'*

And that was that.

And he had dressed and written the note to Eulalia whilst she was still in her bathroom. He had written: *"I'm sorry, Eulalia . . . but there is someone else. There has been for some time. I've got to go. Shaun."* And he had sneaked out and left his clothes; everything. Because that was the easiest way to do it. Easiest for her; for him; and it stopped a lot of questions. Even questions that do not get further than the mind.

That was Mr. Quayle that was.... Come back ... playtime is over.... Goddam Mr. Quayle.

And now he was standing in the yew-tree grove where it was cold on a hot day. He was standing and wondering and trying to think with a mind that was three parts numb with bad liquor and the other part not-so-interested.

But the drink thing was necessary. Or so it seemed. And who the hell was he to argue anyhow.... Nobody ever argued with Mr. Quayle. Well ... not more than about twice.... Not about anything that mattered.

The thing was not fair. Because when you wanted to *be* something; when the time came you would have no guts; no *morale*; no anything. You would be a drunken sot. And if you were not a drunken sot, the time wouldn't come. So anyway you were in hell. Thank you, Mr. Quayle ... thank you very much.... Goddam you, Mr. Quayle, and I hope it keeps fine for you and that you fall in front of a motor bus on a foggy day and to hell with you.

His stomach heaved; he began to feel sick. He stood leaning against a tree waiting for the tremor to pass.

Someone had said of him ... someone ... Ricardo Kerr, he thought it was ... "O'Mara would charm you, would eat and drink with you, converse with you, play cards with you, win money off you, take your girl off you, swear unfailing loyalty to you, and if necessary kill you." That was what Ricky Kerr had said. He wondered what Ricky would say if he could have a look now.

O'Mara realised that he must have a drink. Some sort of drink. Even if it was that lousy firewater that Volanon cooked up in the back room. You had to have a drink when you felt like he did. There was no argument about it.

And that meant that he had to walk round the estuary and go back to the *Garage Volanon* and eat dirt and tell Volanon that he was sorry about last night when he had spat in the face of Tierche, the fish factor. Volanon had been quite peeved about that.

But, anyway, what the hell could *he* do? He had to have some sort of help in the garage and even the drunken O'Mara was better than nothing. Three days a week he could work anyhow . . . sometimes. . . .

He would have to walk round the estuary, and he would sweat some of the liquor out of him, and he might be better. Maybe something was going to happen to-day . . . maybe. It hadn't happened for months and it probably wouldn't, and anyway in about another five weeks he would be all set for the fourth stage, and that was when you started seeing things on the wall.

O'Mara moved slowly out of the yew-tree grove and began to walk along the green fringe that edged the high cliff. On the other side of the estuary he could see Volanon standing at the door of the Café. . . .

O'Mara moved away along the cliff. It would be funny, he thought, if he fell over. And it might save a great deal of trouble. But he wouldn't. No, sir . . . not to-day, sir. . . . No, Mr. Quayle . . . not to-day and goddam you, Mr. Quayle.

The curé in the faded *soutane* came out of the church and walked to the edge of the graveyard. He watched O'Mara as he moved stupidly along the cliff path.

He said: "Poor Philippe . . . poor Philippe. . . ."

CHAPTER TWO
TANGA

O'MARA lay on the ground, his back resting against the white-washed wall that bounded the *Garage Volanon*. He seemed to regard the broken shoe of his right foot with interest, but he did not see the shoe. When a lizard scuttled from a crevice in the sunlit wall, disappeared into another crevice, O'Mara jerked spasmodically. He relaxed after his brain realised that he had really *seen* the lizard.

There had been no work that day. After last night when Volanon had given him the rough edge of his tongue, O'Mara had decided it would be a good thing to remain as sober as possible for a few days; as sober as possible—*possible* being the operative word. He concluded that he did not like lizards. He thought that life would go on in exactly the same way as it was going on at the moment. It would go on like that permanently, except that each day he would be a little more drunken—a little more stupid. And then in the winter it would rain and he would probably die of pneumonia.

O'Mara, who had never considered the possibilities of death, found himself vaguely amused at the thought. He concluded that there was never a chance of anything happening; that he was part of a picture that was constant; that would continue. A rather dreary picture in the beautiful setting created by the sunlight which flooded this side of the estuary; which illuminated the red roof and white walls of the garage.

And then it happened.

The Typhoon car shot round the corner out of the narrow main street of the little fishing village. The driver was expert, for the car was long and at the speed at which it was going it was necessary to skid the car. It came round the corner at a good thirty-five; accelerated down the dirt road that led towards the arm of the estuary; slowed down; stopped directly outside the garage.

O'Mara did not move. The pain had come in his left arm. His left leg was beginning to tremble. These were the usual symptoms for this time of the day. They called it all sorts of names. A doctor from a neighbouring town had been nice enough to describe it as a sort of false *angina*. Actually, it was drink, more drink, and Caporal cigarettes—lots of them. That and not eating and nerves.

O'Mara regarded the broken shoe on his right foot with even more interest. Now he felt a little cold. Supposing this was it! Was he good enough? Had he got the guts? Out of the corner of his eye he watched the car. The door opened and a woman's leg emerged—a beautiful leg; superbly clad; the stocking of the sheerest silk. O'Mara knew the leg. He thought: My God . . . it's happened! Tanga!

So it was to be she. Tanga de Sarieux, whom he had met once and remembered often. He remembered the slow, quiet voice, the delightful French accent.

She got out of the car. She walked towards the garage. She disappeared through the open sliding doors into the cool shadows. She walked with the supreme aplomb, the grace of carriage, that was part of her make-up. O'Mara thought: What a hell of a woman! He found himself trembling a little.

The afternoon was very quiet. There was no breeze from the sea. There was the buzzing and droning of flies—the noises that come with the hot summer; that make the silence more definite. Inside the garage, O'Mara could hear Tanga's cool, clear voice demanding attention from somebody. He looked at the car. The front near-side tyre was nearly flat. So that was it!

Some minutes passed. Tanga came out of the garage. She walked towards the car, followed by Volanon. Volanon was fat, greasy and sweating. His stained linen trousers were tied round his middle with a piece of cord. His belly sagged over the top.

He said: "If that's all it is, Madame, we'll soon fix it for you. If I can get this drunken imbecile to work." He looked towards O'Mara. He called: "Hi, Philippe . . . come along, my drunken sot. Change this wheel. The spare is on the back."

Tanga looked at O'Mara. She said coldly: "Do you think he could change a wheel? He looks drunk to me."

Volanon shrugged his shoulders. He said: "Madame has reason. He is drunk. He has never been sober. He has everything—a variety of maladies. One looks at him and imagines that also he has the *cafard*. But always he is able to work after a style."

Tanga said: "Why don't *you* change the tyre?"

Volanon said with dignity: "But, Madame, I am the proprietor."

Tanga began to laugh. Volanon, a shadow crossing his face and with a final scowl at O'Mara, turned; went towards the garage. Inside the doors, he turned. He called back:

"Madame is requested to pay me—not to give money to the drunken Philippe."

Tanga nodded. O'Mara could hear the rope-soled shoes of Volanon pattering away into the recesses of the garage. He planned to get up. He got up. He got up by the process of turning over on his knees, pushing himself up into a kneeling position, putting his two hands on the top of the low wall and pulling. With difficulty he achieved a vertical position. He stood for a moment leaning against the wall; then walked slowly towards the car. She looked at him with distaste.

She said: "The jack is in the back. There is a lock on the spare wheel. Here is the key. Also I am in a hurry. You will be quick?"

O'Mara said: "But of course. That is understood." He continued more formally: "Madame, speed is the essence of our work in this supreme and high-class organisation. It will not take me very long to change the wheel."

She said: "Good."

O'Mara went on: "But it would seem to me that you have a puncture. If you want the puncture repaired before you go on—and I would advise you to have it repaired—it will take a little time."

She asked: "How much time?"

He shrugged his shoulders. "A half an hour," he said.

Tanga looked across the estuary. She looked across to the other side, to the green hill with the tiny church and graveyard on the top.

She said: "There is a villa somewhere in this place called *Cote d'Azur*. I believe it is not far. I might go there and return in an hour to collect the car. I take it that the puncture would be mended by then?"

O'Mara said: "Definitely." He was leaning against the bonnet of the Typhoon, looking at Tanga. He looked at her with eyes that were hungry but inoffensive. He looked at her in the way that the old O'Mara could look at a woman and not annoy her—with a peculiar mixture of humility and insolence, admiration and question.

He looked for what seemed to him a long time. He thought: So it's going to be this one. He realised—as he had never realised before; even before the drink business had become necessary—that she had everything—beauty, intelligence, and that peculiar but supremely necessary *nous* that was an essential part of the make-up of an *artiste* in the odd profession to which she belonged; to which he belonged—or did he?

She wore a tunic and skirt of buttercup colour crêpe-de-chine, and her mouth was the colour of raspberries. Her face was beautiful and with an alluring dignity that belonged essentially to her.

In her ears she wore small amber flower ear-rings that matched her clothes. Her hair was black, dressed in a page-boy bob for driving; tied with an amber ribbon. Her shoes were of white buckskin, and she wore yellow buckskin driving gauntlets.

O'Mara thought to himself that if you saw this woman once or twice you would forget all about Eulalia. He thought that Eulalia would fade into the remote past. That was how he felt at that moment.

He said: "I think that would be an excellent idea, Madame. I should not have to hurry about repairing the puncture."

He went to the back of the car. He returned after a minute or two with the jack. He sat down on the ground; pushed the jack under the front axle; began to turn the jack handle. He turned it slowly.

Tanga said: "I am interested in this puncture. Is it a puncture or do you think there is a defective valve on the tyre?"

O'Mara said: "Let us examine this proposition." Now the wheel was free on the ground. He rolled himself on to his knees, crawled round and sat in front of the wheel. With fingers that were trembling he began to unscrew the valve cover.

He said: "It is very stiff, Madame, or perhaps my fingers are not as good as they used to be."

She looked over the estuary towards the church. She said softly, in English, with her own peculiar and fascinating accent: "Listen, my delightful, drunken sweet. I think you are wonderful." Then in a louder tone, in French: "Valves are always stiff if they have not been unscrewed. Besides, it is your nasty fine Breton dust which clogs them." She said in English under her breath: "I think you are superb. You are *so* drunk and you are getting fat and paunchy. What has happened to my beautiful O'Mara?"

O'Mara muttered a wicked word. His fingers were still fumbling at the valve.

She went on softly: "A certain Taudrille will telephone at exactly six o'clock. You understand? *This is* it, my friend. At exactly six o'clock Taudrille will telephone. You understand?"

He nodded. He said: "Yes. Volanon will not be here at six. I shall take the call. Of course he knows the number."

She said: "Of course, my sweet fool." She was smiling and still looking over the estuary towards the church. She dropped the words at him. He tried not to look at her.

He asked quietly: "And then?"

She shrugged her shoulders almost imperceptibly. She said: "Then it is up to you. Things begin to move. Are you good enough, my delightful, my clever, my drunken Shaun?"

He said: "God knows—I don't. But I have a bottle of coramine. When I take a double dose it pulls me together for quite a bit."

She smiled. Now her eyes were wandering round the estuary. She seemed vaguely interested in the sunlight playing on the water.

She said: "You will need that, my sweet. You will need something to put a jerk into you, especially"—she laughed very softly—"if Taudrille is not able to arrive exactly on time."

O'Mara said: "What the hell does that mean?"

She shrugged her shoulders.

O'Mara could hear the plop-plop of Volanon's rope-soled shoes. Now the valve was off. He said: "Madame, it is not the valve. You have a puncture." He got up; went to the back of the car; produced tools. He took the hub cap off the wheel; began to unscrew the screws.

Volanon came to the door of the garage. He stood watching O'Mara.

Tanga moved away. She said to Volanon: "I have friends here at a villa called the *Cote d'Azur*. Is it far? I propose to go and see them; to come back in an hour's time. By that time this one tells me that the puncture will be mended."

Volanon said: "Excellent, Madame. In an hour's time, I have no doubt the no-good Philippe will have done the job. But as I shall not be here when you return perhaps you would like to settle now. Then I will tell you where the *Cote d'Azur* is. It is not far."

Out of the corner of his eye O'Mara saw her give some money to Volanon. They spoke for a few moments whilst he told her the way to the Villa. She walked away. Volanon watched her retreating form. He came over; stood above O'Mara.

He said: "There is a woman, *mon vieux*. It is a long time since I have seen a woman as lovely as that one. Does it not make your mouth water?"

O'Mara said: "It means nothing to me."

Volanon nodded. "See that you mend her puncture with care," he said. "Don't make a mess of that. She may be a good customer."

He went back into the garage.

O'Mara took the heavy wheel by the spokes; pulled it off. The process pleased him. He was doing something definite. He said to himself: So Taudrille will phone at six o'clock. Now maybe this is all over. Maybe there will be some life again. He trundled the wheel away; leaned it against the low wall. He was surprised to find that he was humming to himself.

It was half-past three in the afternoon.

Mr. Quayle—whose business was nobody's business—who was just past fifty; inclined to be bald—sat at his desk in his room in the offices of the International Refrigeration Company, in Pall Mall, and considered that life was just as tragically ridiculous as it had been during the war years. If, he thought, the tragedies were not so numerous, the effects were much the same. The effects were possibly more serious because human life in peace-time is held, for some odd and quite unaccountable reason, to be more precious than in time of war.

This foible—for Mr. Quayle considered it to be a foible—was not helpful to him in his rather peculiar business—a business which specialised in the lives of many people and was, therefore, concerned, on occasion, with the sudden departure from this earth of individuals whose *raison d'être* would seem to have disappeared.

He considered two lists which lay on the desk before him. They were lists of names. A long list and a short one. The long list represented the number of operatives in Mr. Quayle's rather peculiar organisation who had died or been reported missing in the war years; the shorter list represented those who had merely "disappeared" since.

The desk telephone buzzed. He picked up the receiver. A dulcet voice said: "Mr. Quayle, there are four furniture vans from the Office of Works outside. They seem to have an idea that we're going to move?"

Quayle said: "They're perfectly right, Myra. We *are* going to move. Tell the man in charge that they will begin to clear the Company's offices at five-thirty. The vans must be loaded by six. They will then go to Golden Square and park on the west side of the square. A foreman from the Office of Works will meet them there with a new driver for each van. He will have his instructions."

She said: "Very well, Mr. Quayle."

He asked: "Where is Ernest Guelvada?"

"At home," she said. "I telephoned him this morning. I told him that I should probably be ringing him again."

Quayle said: "Tell him to be here at a quarter past four." He hung up the receiver.

He picked up the long list. Behind the formal typescript he saw the faces represented by the names. There was Eversley—the young man with the fondness for music. Eversley had been unlucky. He hadn't lasted long. The Nazis had got him in 1944. But he was lucky in a way. He had been shot. And there was Mrs. Gwendoline Ermine—a plump good-figured woman who had spoken German so well, who looked so like a certain type of German woman and who was so pretty and gentle.

Quayle had heard that Mrs. Ermine hadn't died quite so quickly. They'd been rather unkind to her. And there was the clever French girl, Mavrique. They'd got Mavrique in Paris and put her through it and she'd talked quite a lot—because she *had* to talk—everyone had a breaking point—and they'd got on to Michaelson and Duborg through her. He'd lost them too. Good types those two.

He produced a cigarette lighter. He burned the long list; watched the grey ashes settle in the glass ash-tray. And that was that. Mr. Quayle sighed. It seemed a great pity to him that all those people—some of them very nice people—should finish like that. He thought that most of them *had* finished like that. He remembered some of them. . . .

He picked up the short list; regarded it carefully. Then he burned it and put it in the ash-tray with the other ashes. He wasn't at all pleased about the short list. The long one represented the fortunes of war but the short one was different.

Mr. Quayle thought he was going to do something about that.

He began to arrange a chessboard in his mind. But the pieces were not Kings and Queens and Knights and Castles and Pawns. The pieces were men and women, and you could call them just what you liked. He began to arrange the new set-up for the next "game," picking his people in his mind; arranging what was to happen as a result of what had happened.

He thought for a long time. He smoked a lot of cigarettes and started many fresh series of thoughts, working away from different theoretic bases; trying out new combinations of ideas but always thinking ahead of the situation which he had already created; which should now be arriving almost at its crucial point. A situation which had already arrived at the point where the not-so-good, the drunken, Philippe Garenne was engaged in finding a puncture in an inner tube at a small and somewhat dilapidated garage on the estuary at Saint-Brieuc.

After a while he turned his mind to the present. He was certain of one thing. There was only one man who could function in the little set piece that Mr. Quayle had in his mind. A man who was clever enough, single-minded enough, to function in a manner that might be considered adequate.

Guelvada . . . that was the man. Ernest Guelvada—otherwise known as Ernie—the man who had been a Free Belgian during the war; who was now an Englishman by virtue of his services. Guelvada, who seemed so happy, and whose heart was filled with an unutterable bitterness against everything Nazi . . . with a bitterness that occasionally overflowed into his guts with results that were sometimes overpowering for the subject of his acerbity.

Guelvada, thought Quayle, had a sufficiency of hatred to make him quite merciless if and when an entire lack of mercy was necessary; enough brains to be opportunist when the situation required a quick change of front; enough virility and manliness to simulate—at least to simulate if not actually to experience—a certain weakness where a woman was concerned—*if* the woman was attractive enough and if the "weakness" did not interfere—or seemed not to interfere—with the business immediately at hand.

The man, thought Quayle, must be Guelvada.

The subject of Mr. Quayle's deliberations turned from a sunlit Piccadilly into St. James's Street. Guelvada was short, very well dressed after the fashion of those good-class tailoring designs which one sees in tailors' shops but of which nobody—except Mr. Guelvada—ever takes the slightest notice. His face was round. His attitude was one of complacent good humour—an attitude which belied his feelings. Within he was not particularly happy. During the war years he had lived in atmospheres so peculiar, so varied and, even for him, so exciting, that the anti-climax of peace—even if that anti-climax were not *quite* so decided as a lot of people would wish—was inclined to be boring.

He was half-way down St. James's Street before he began to think about Mr. Quayle. This, thought Ernest, would be the pay-off.

Everything was over and finished. Ministers, diplomats and "experts" were meeting in all sorts of places to decide the fate of the world. There would be no more shooting in dark corners; no more sombre and slowly flowing rivers carrying on their bosoms a quiescent corpse. No more knives in dark alleyways; no more tense quiet inquisitions where somebody was made to talk because their talking was necessary to the safety of many others. All these things, thought Guelvada, were passing slowly—if they had not already passed.

He did not like that—not at all. It was as if someone was removing a well-loved woman from his arms, and he powerless to stop the process. Guelvada carried his mind back for a few years—to 1940—to the not very pleasant picture which the body of the young woman whom he then adored had presented after the enemy had finished with her. He licked his lips. Since then he had been settling old scores, delighting in the process. Now it seemed that there would be more scores to settle. He considered this to be unfortunate.

He turned into Pall Mall. A little way down the street outside the offices—Quayle's offices—the International Refrigeration Company—stood two large furniture vans. Guelvada sighed. His guess had been right. This was the pay-off. He turned into the entrance to the offices; went up in the lift to the first floor. He pushed open the door of the main office; walked in. The girl at the switchboard—a demure blonde—said: "Good afternoon . . .?"

Guelvada said in perfect English: "Good afternoon. My name is Ernest Guelvada. To see Mr. Quayle."

She said: "Will you go straight in, Mr. Guelvada, please."

Guelvada crossed the office; pushed open the oak door on the far side; closed it behind him. On the other side of the room, behind the large desk set at an angle to the corner, Quayle was sitting, smoking a cigarette. He looked up.

He said: "Hello, Ernie."

Guelvada said: "Hello—or possibly farewell. Mr. Quayle, I see the furniture vans are outside."

Quayle said: "You're disappointed, are you?"

Guelvada shrugged his shoulders. "Why not?" he said. "Now what is there left for *me*?"

Quayle smiled. His large round face, beneath the almost bald head, was benign. He said: "I shouldn't worry too much about that if I were you."

Guelvada said: "Well, I'm glad to hear it. I was only guessing. When I saw the furniture vans outside . . ."

Quayle interrupted: "The deduction doesn't follow. Anybody can hire furniture vans. Sit down."

Guelvada sat down. Quayle got up, stubbed out his cigarette; began to walk up and down the office. Guelvada sat quietly. He was wondering.

After a little while Quayle said: "The thing you've got to understand, Ernest, is this. The war is officially over. I said officially. Unofficially, all sorts of strange things are happening in a world which is still sitting on a keg of dynamite. The world wants peace badly, but there are quite a lot of people in it who don't think like that. There are lots of opportunities for them to-day. You understand?"

Guelvada said: "You're telling me. I understand perfectly."

"Very well," said Quayle. "It will be obvious to you that the fact that the war is over must affect the technique of rather peculiar organisations like our own—organisations which were able to function in one way whilst the war was on. Now it's got to be in another way. We've got to be a great deal more careful. That means that operatives will have to take more chances."

Guelvada said softly: "One has always taken chances."

"I know," said Quayle. "But there are chances and chances." He smiled at Guelvada. "I'd hate to see you hanged," he said casually.

There was a silence; then Guelvada said: "I get it. Before, one had a chance of a bullet or a knife in the back or something perhaps not so pleasant, but one was never *officially* hanged. Now there's even a chance of that."

Quayle said: "Exactly."

Guelvada drew a breath of cigarette smoke into his lungs. He said: "A new experience in any event—possibly amusing. I've been shot and stabbed before. I have never yet been hanged."

Quayle sat down behind the desk. He said: "It will be quite obvious to you that there are organisations, similar to the one I control, working for our late enemies. No one has ever put their finger on those organisations. We might have known of their existence; found counter-measures. But when the war was finished they went underground. There are few clues as to what happened to them. One can only see them by the things they do. One set of war criminals has been tried and executed, but the people I'm talking about are probably the best types of our original enemies. They took all the chances we took. Not very nice people possibly, but very brave and now inclined, possibly, to be more desperate than ever."

Guelvada said: "Of course they've got to *do* something. If they do nothing they haven't a chance, so they must do something. They don't care what they do because they feel like rats in a trap."

Quayle nodded. He said: "There was a man called Rozanski—a rather peculiar type. Rozanski was a junior officer in a crack German Cavalry Regiment at the beginning of the 1914-18 war—a very good officer, I believe. He had an accident—injured his left leg.

He wasn't able to ride any more. Of course he could have transferred to some other branch of the service but he didn't like the idea. They gave him an alternative. He went into one of the original German Intelligence Services. He had an aptitude for the work. He liked it. Eventually, after the last war, he was transferred to one of the external German Espionage organisations. He did very well with that. When it looked as if the Hitler *régime* was coming to an end, that Germany was beaten, you know what happened. Most of the internal and external espionage units who weren't known to anybody—not even to the armed forces, Intelligence Services or even the Gestapo—went underground. There were no records for the Allies to find because there *weren't* any records. It wouldn't matter if our people arrested Rozanski tomorrow. They couldn't prove anything against him. You understand?"

Guelvada said: "Yes. You *know* but you can't prove anything."

Quayle said: "If I could I shouldn't want to prove anything. That wouldn't help me." He went on: "Since peace has been officially declared I've lost thirty-seven agents in Central Europe, in circumstances where I shouldn't have lost one. Nobody knows who's responsible. The Control Governments don't know. The Germans don't know. Nobody knows, but we can guess a lot."

Guelvada said: "You want this Rozanski?"

Quayle said: "Yes. Rozanski has been getting about Europe in a very big way. He gets false papers and passports with the greatest of ease. He's well supplied with money. A great deal of money has been coming from somewhere. Maybe they had a *cache* when the war was finished. That's another thing one would like to find out."

Guelvada said: "Mr. Quayle, do you know where this Rozanski is operating at the moment?"

Quayle said: "I've an idea. In any event, I think a situation is going to develop. Rozanski's getting on. He must be fifty-six or fifty-seven by now. A man's nerve doesn't last all the time and he's been through a lot."

Guelvada said nothing. Quayle walked up and down the long office for two or three minutes before he went on.

Then: "I'll give you such information as we have or as much as I think you ought to know," he said. "I'm certain that Rozanski knows about you and your existence. A lot of people know about you, Ernie"—he smiled—"in Europe, I mean. Somehow I'm going to try to get the idea into Rozanski's head that we're after him; that I've put you in to finish him; to use that funny little Swedish knife of yours, or one of your other 'methods'; to use that technique you employed so adequately when the war was on. I'm going to try to get that idea into his head. I think I can do that."

Guelvada said: "Yes. And then?"

"Then," said Quayle, "I want you to get on his tail. Quite obviously, Rozanski will be aware that we cannot finish him off as we might have finished him off in the war. He knows we've got to be more careful about it. In other words, he will realise that before you can deal with him you'll have to have a proper set-up in which you *can* deal with him. He'll realise that it's got to look like an accident or something like that. He'll know that all the time you're trying to create the circumstances in which you can finish him and leave the job looking, as I say, like an accident. The result will be he'll be watching you like a cat. If you play your cards in the way I think you will—and you're a good actor, Ernie—I think Rozanski is going to get very scared."

Guelvada said: "And then?"

"When a man gets scared," said Quayle, "he does all sorts of strange things. He begins to give himself away. Especially when he's been lucky enough to get through the years of war doing the dangerous work that he's been doing. Perhaps he finds that life is still sweet for *him,* even if he resorts to desperate measures against others."

Guelvada nodded. "Maybe," he said.

"Go back to your place, Ernest," said Quayle. "I'll send you a chit to-night telling you exactly what you're to do. Read it and burn it."

Guelvada asked: "Am I working with anybody?"

"Yes," said Quayle. "You're very lucky in one way because you'll be working with a woman who is extremely clever. I think she's one of the most superb operatives that I've ever known. Beautiful too. Her name is Tanga. She is the Comtesse de Sarieux."

Guelvada said: "So she's clever?"

"Very clever," said Quayle. "It's necessary that she should be. I suppose you remember O'Mara?"

"Do I remember!" said Guelvada. "How could one forget O'Mara? What a man! Is he in on this? This sounds like a wonderful team. Everyone very beautiful or very expert . . . hey?"

Quayle said seriously: "O'Mara is in on this. Probably he wishes he wasn't." He went on: "I've known for a long time that the man Rozanski has been operating in France. The Second Bureau had a line on him but I asked them not to do anything about it. So they left him alone. He's been doing more or less what he liked. He seems to have been concentrating on *my* people more or less. Rozanski can be absolutely cold-blooded if he wants to. He's one of those people who believe in anything they do. He puts everything he's got into the job. You probably know the type."

Guelvada said: "I know . . . very difficult people to deal with. Very *formidable* . . . complete bastards actually . . . not at all nice. . . ."

"Quite so," said Quayle. "It seemed to me a rather peculiar coincidence that four of my people disappeared within a circle of about thirty miles in diameter with the centre point of the diameter line on Gouarec in Brittany."

Guelvada said: "How interesting . . . rather peculiar that. . . ."

"In a way yes," said Quayle. "You mean, I take it, that this betokens a certain carelessness on their part?"

The Belgian shrugged his shoulders. "That or a lack of real organisation," he said. "Incidentally . . . just now you said that this Rozanski seemed to have been concentrating on people in this organisation. This seems to me to be strange. The French must still be working. They *must* be. There is so much to clear up. The Second Bureau . . ."

"Precisely," said Quayle. "But the French don't tell us what their people are doing unless they want a contact for a special reason. Neither do we tell the French unless we require assistance."

"I see," said Guelvada. "Now I see. . . . So it seems that this Rozanski knows about your organisation in that part of the world. He knows nothing about the French because he is not concerned with them. Probably because he knows nothing about their operations, but he knows about yours. For some reason he has discovered something and . . ."

Quayle nodded. "Exactly," he said. "Rozanski found out something *somehow*. And he started from there. Possibly he has someone behind him; possibly he is working on his own in a last desperate effort to pull something out of the bag—something *very* special—before he hands in his pay-check and goes to the place where all good Nazis go when they've had it."

Guelvada said: "Of course you are right." He smiled. "But then I believe you are always right. I do not think you make mistakes, Mr. Quayle."

Quayle said: "I don't like making mistakes. When I do, somebody usually gets it in the neck. That doesn't make *me* feel any better about it. It doesn't make it any easier for me because it's someone else."

He looked at the little pile of grey ashes in the ash-tray. He went on: "Rozanski knew something. He must have picked up something from *somewhere*. He started from that and scored one or two minor successes. You remember a man called Parlass who worked with you in Belgium during the early part of the war?"

Guelvada nodded.

"Parlass was killed. His body was found under a train some twenty-five miles from Gouarec; then there was another man and a woman called Desperes—a very nice woman—and a girl named Lissol—an Irish girl. It seemed to me that Rozanski knew something. Therefore in order to get a little better acquainted with his technique it became necessary for me to give him something else to work on."

Guelvada smiled. He said: "I understand . . . at least I *think* I understand. You gave him *someone*?"

Quayle nodded. "I gave him Shaun Aloysius O'Mara," he said with a wry smile. "In a bag."

Guelvada said quietly: "My God . . . *not* O'Mara!"

Quayle shrugged his shoulders. "I *had* to," he said. "It had to be someone who was very good."

"I know," said Guelvada. "I understand."

"We arranged a set-up a long time ago," said Quayle. "The idea was that O'Mara was to go to the bad. It was quite on the cards that we should pay him off after the war; give him a good gratuity and let him go. They could believe that. O'Mara went to Paris and spent a lot of money and gambled and drank like a fish. Those were my instructions—to go absolutely to the bad; to go quite—or almost quite—rotten. You understand that O'Mara has got such a weird pride of achievement that even if he were rotten with drink he'd still do the job—even if he had to crucify himself to do it."

Guelvada said: "I have always understood that O'Mara was definitely a man. But definitely . . ."

"He got himself into a lot of trouble in Paris," said Quayle. "He was supreme. He was picked up by the police two or three times. One or two high up knew who he was and what he had done for me in the war. They got in touch with me. I told them that so far as I was concerned O'Mara was out; that he no longer had anything to do with me and that they could send him to Devil's Island for all I cared."

Guelvada said: "Very good . . . very sound technique."

"O'Mara went from bad to worse," said Quayle. "Or so it seemed. He was kicked out of half a dozen jobs. He got other jobs. He got thrown into jail and came out again. But always he worked nearer and nearer to Brittany. He knows the country. He got a job on a farm and stole from the farmer. He went into a hospital with near D.T.s. I tell you he's been amazing. He's even surprised *me*. . . ."

Guelvada said quietly: "O'Mara was always the supreme *artiste*. Always a thing must be done right . . . right to the end."

"I hope it won't be the end," said Quayle brusquely. "Anyhow . . . O'Mara picked up a job on the estuary near Saint-Brieuc. He helps a man named Volanon. Volanon is a bit of a drunk himself so he's not too ill disposed to O'Mara, who he thinks is one no-good Philippe Garenne with a semi-criminal record. Volanon has a small garage on the estuary. He pays O'Mara practically nothing.

He gives him food of a sort and enough bad liquor to keep him drunk enough to stay on the job. . . ."

Guelvada said: "I am beginning to understand. *Rozanski knew O'Mara.*"

"Right," said Quayle. "Rozanski knew O'Mara. He *had* to know that O'Mara was working for me during the war. It seemed to me that sooner or later Rozanski would get on to O'Mara—especially as he was using the district as a stamping ground—or perhaps as a stamping *out* ground," said Quayle with a wry smile. "I concluded that he would get on to O'Mara and would discover the condition he was in. He would do something about it. He would get at O'Mara before he finished him. He would certainly finish him off for old time's sake, and because O'Mara worked for me during the war. But first he would make him talk, and it isn't difficult to make a drunken sot talk. . . ."

Guelvada said very quietly: "My God, Mr. Quayle, you can be very tough. But *tough.*"

"This is a tough game," said Quayle. "We haven't time for sentiment. I've never professed to be running a girls' school anyhow. . . ."

"No," said Guelvada. "But certainly not a *girls'* school. . . . My God. . . . *No!* But I should like to ask a question."

Quayle waited.

"This Rozanski is obviously no fool," said Guelvada. "Therefore if he comes to the conclusion that O'Mara is merely a drunken sot who once worked for you, whilst he might, for old time's sake, finish him off, I do not see why he should bother to make such a no-good specimen talk. Obviously, O'Mara, being a no-good specimen thrown over by you, would know nothing. What could he say. . . even under the most refined torture . . . what could he tell? Surely Rozanski would not *expect* O'Mara, in present circumstances, to know anything."

Quayle said casually: "Rozanski would *know* O'Mara knew *one* thing. *He would know that O'Mara knows who I am.*"

Guelvada whistled quietly. "I see it. You are putting Rozanski on to you. You are taking that chance. I see. You think that Rozanski will get at O'Mara and make him talk; that O'Mara will crack; that he will tell them who you are—*you* the centre of the organisation; the very heart-beat of the whole thing. O'Mara will tell them who you are and where you are. . . ."

"Right," said Quayle. "That is what I think will happen, and then Rozanski will *have* to do something about it. He will have to make his final play—for me. To do this he must show his hand—somehow . . . to someone . . . some time. . . . Then we get him."

Guelvada said: "Yes . . . a magnificent plan. And O'Mara?"

Quayle said: "You can't make omelettes without breaking eggs." He looked at his watch. "Go home. I will send you instructions in the usual way this evening. You must be in France to-morrow morning. You might have a very interesting time." He smiled at Guelvada.

Guelvada got up. He said: "It sounds as if I am going to have a *very* interesting time. I hope to be seeing you again soon."

Quayle was still smiling. "You will," he said. "I *hope*."

Guelvada went out.

It was five o'clock. Tanga came out of the bathroom at the Villa Cote d'Azur. She was wearing an eau-de-nil crêpe-de-chine robe and sandals. She tied the belt of the robe as she walked down the short passageway from the bathroom to the sitting-room. Yvette, the maid—tall, raw-boned, hard-faced, intelligent—stood by the window, the telephone receiver in her hand.

Tanga sat down; crossed her legs; took a cigarette from the box on the table; lit it. Every movement was charming, imbued with an unstudied grace.

She said: "Well, Yvette?"

The maid said: "In a minute, Madame. I have spoken to the *Sûreté National*. They say they will get the local exchange to give you a cut-out call to the number. They say there is no possibility of anyone overhearing."

Tanga smiled. She said: "Yes?"

Yvette spoke into the receiver. She said: "They say they will call back here." She hung up the receiver; stood looking at her mistress.

A thin stream of smoke issued from Tanga's raspberry mouth. She watched it as it widened, spreading itself on the air; disappearing. She said: "Well . . . tell me about it, Yvette. What's been going on? Has it been amusing?"

The woman shrugged her shoulders. "How could it be amusing, Madame," she said, "in a place like this? In any event, I am not particularly amused with life. I have never been since those swine killed my husband."

Tanga said: "I know. I feel sorry about that. Husbands always seem so much more attractive in retrospect. Did you love him so much when he was alive?"

The maid shrugged her shoulders. She smiled a little ruefully. "Perhaps you're right, Madame," she said. "Perhaps when he was alive I was not so fond of him as I think I am now that he is no longer with me." She folded her hands in front of her—thin, strong hands.

She went on: "I came here and took the Villa. It was understood that I was housekeeper to Monsieur de Chervasse and his wife. That fact was established in the minds of the people here when he and she came down and stayed for two weeks. You will remember, Madame, you arranged that."

Tanga nodded.

"When they went I was supposed to remain here in charge of the Villa. Nothing very much happens here and so there is gossip. The fishermen do not like the ordinary people of the town. Always there is a great deal of talk, but I made a speaking acquaintance with a Monsieur Tierche who is the local fish factor. He likes to talk. Very often he would stop his cart here in the morning and I would give him a glass of byrrh. He used to lean up against the post of the gate and talk. I learned about Philippe Garenne."

Tanga asked nonchalantly: "What did they say, Vyette?"

The maid went on: "They said he was drinking himself to death. I can believe that too. I have seen him. It seems a pity. At one time he must have been a fine man Often he is found in the streets blind drunk. Volanon, who employs him, is himself a bit of a drunkard."

Tanga said: "Yes?"

The telephone bell rang. The maid took up the receiver. After a moment she said: "It is the English call, Madame."

She put the instrument down; went away quietly.

Tanga crossed the room; took up the receiver.

Quayle's voice said: "Good afternoon, Madame la Comtesse."

Tanga laughed softly. She said: "Good afternoon."

Quayle asked: "How are the weather conditions in your part of the world? Do you think there is going to be good flying weather?"

Tanga laughed again. She said: "On the contrary, I think a storm—whether it's going to be a large or a small storm I cannot say—is imminent."

Quayle said quickly: "That suggestion is based on information, I take it? Perhaps you heard something from a meteorological expert?"

Tanga said: "I had some information. I had some information from a gentleman who might be called a meteorological expert—a Mr. Epps in Paris. Apparently Mr. Epps had heard from somebody."

"From Taudrille?" Quayle suggested.

"Exactly," said Tanga. "Monsieur Taudrille suggested that there might be a little storm; that it might break somewhere in the region of six o'clock to-night; that if such a possibility were to seem imminent someone would be called on the telephone."

Quayle said: "Do you think the recipient of the call—if it comes—is in a fit condition to take notice?"

"Definitely," she said. "I must say, having regard to all things, that I have an admiration for the recipient."

Quayle said: "We all have. Do you think he would be able to weather any storm that broke?"

She shrugged her shoulders. "I would say that that depends," she said, "on the ferocity or otherwise of the storm."

"Excellent," said Quayle. "Everything seems to be moving very nicely. Are you comfortable?"

She said: "Yes. I am here at the *Villa Cote d'Azur* with Yvette, my maid. It seems that Monsieur and Madame de Chervasse have sub-let the villa to me for a month. I have a car here. A puncture is being mended at the moment at the *Garage Volanon* on the estuary. I shall go back there very shortly and get it, if it is ready."

Quayle said: "You'd better let me know, if you can, what happens after the storm has broken."

She said: "*I* would like some indication of what might happen after this storm. I am not quite certain of the atmosphere."

Quayle laughed. He said: "Neither am I, but I think it quite possible that following a good storm the atmosphere might be extremely close—humid—and with possibilities of further thunderstorms."

She said softly: "I see."

He went on: "I expect you are looking forward to your visitor— the gentleman you have asked to the *Cote d'Azur.*"

Tanga raised her eyebrows. She said: "So I have asked a visitor? How exciting." She laughed—the laugh was barely a murmur.

Quayle said: "Yes. The gentleman whom you met in Paris some time ago—last year, I think. Possibly you've forgotten that you asked him to spend a week or so with you at the Villa. You remember you told me that he was a most interesting character. Surely you remember the name—Mr. Ernest Guelvada."

Tanga raised her eyebrows again. She smiled a little. She twisted one corner of her beautiful mouth. She said: "Oh, thank you for reminding me. But I am not at all sorry that Mr. Guelvada has been able to come. That's excellent."

Quayle said: "Quite. He's not at all a bad sort of man to have about the place in stormy weather. Well, *au revoir,* Madame la Comtesse. My good wishes to you."

She said: "Thank you. And to you."

She hung up the receiver; went to her bedroom. Yvette was standing by the dressing-table.

Tanga said: "You'd better get me out a linen coat and skirt, Yvette. I'm going down to the garage to get the car."

"Very good, Madame. What happens? Is one permitted to know?"

Tanga shrugged her shoulders. Her eyes were smiling and casual; almost disinterested. She took her cigarette from her mouth and crushed it in the ash-tray. Her fingers were long and white and strong.

"*I* don't know what's going to happen," she said, as softly as if she were speaking to herself. "God knows . . . and He is not likely to vouchsafe us any information at the moment."

Yvette shrugged her shoulders jerkily. She said: "No . . . but if it were a man, Madame . . . if it were a man you'd find a way to make him talk. I have no doubt. . . ."

Tanga said dryly: "Neither have I."

She sat down at the dressing-table.

O'Mara sat on the edge of the dilapidated bed which stood against the wall of the small and filthy room in which he slept above the front entrance to the *Garage Volanon*. From where he sat he could see, through the cleaner corner of the window, the back half of the Typhoon which stood outside the garage where he had left it after repairing the puncture. He sat looking at the car, wondering what the next move was going to be. The pain in his left arm had gone, but his legs were not very steady. He got up and tried them out. He walked across the room with steps which were firmer than he thought they would be.

O'Mara began to think of himself as he had been before he had started on this adventure at the estuary. He wondered how long it would take him to get back into that condition. He walked to the window; leaned against the wall; stood looking through the dirty pane.

Tanga came down the narrow road and into his view. O'Mara watched her walking. It seemed to him that she moved with a certain charming detachment; as if she were not particularly interested in the process of walking in this mundane world.

She walked round the Typhoon looking at the tyres. Then she went to the back of the car and removed the key of the boot which was in the lock where O'Mara had left it. Then she got into the car, backed it towards the garage, swung the wheel; drove off towards the main street.

Quayle, thought O'Mara, was a hell of a picker. Always he managed to find the right people for the situation. He wondered just what sort of position this woman occupied in the Quayle scheme of things; just what she had to do with everything; just what she would have to do with him. She was a hell of a woman, O'Mara thought. A woman who could start a hell of a lot of trouble.

He realised that, except for the wives of such fishermen as were married, the rather extraordinary servant-maid who looked after the Tierche establishment, and Yvette du Clos—the woman who was the housekeeper to the de Chervasses at the *Cote d'Azur*—to whom he had spoken once or twice, he had not seen a woman who mattered for months. In any event, he thought, you could go a long while and a great distance in any country in the world without seeing such a woman as this one.

O'Mara moved away from the window. He went out of the room, along the little passageway to the room where Volanon slept. He pushed open the door; went in. The small clock which stood on the chair in the corner, which was the only unbroken piece in the room, showed him that it was twenty minutes to six. He stood against the doorpost looking at the clock, considering facts. If he took a double dose of coramine now on an empty stomach, it would be in his blood-stream in fifteen minutes. A double dose of coramine usually jerked his mind into activity and pushed a certain amount of co-ordination into his body. That meant to say he would be on his toes certainly by five to six. But the effects of the coramine would not last for long—certainly not for more than three-quarters of an hour. He wondered if that would be long enough. He thought that it was damned unfair that he had to go into things which were unknown to him, to weigh up possibilities of which he had little knowledge. He thought he would have to do something about that.

He went back to his room, poured out some cold water from the cracked jug into the worst-cracked basin, sluiced his head and face. He dried himself on a not-too-clean towel; walked over to the bed; pulled up the badly stuffed mattress; fumbled about beneath; produced the bottle of coramine and the case with the injection and the syringe. He went back to the washstand, poured the liquid that remained in the bottle into a cup. He held the cup up. He said with a rueful grin: "Here's damned good luck to you, O'Mara."

He drank the stuff; then he drank a little water. He filled the syringe from the ampoule. Then, holding the filled syringe in his right hand, he fumbled in his pocket for a vesta, struck it on his trouser leg, held the syringe needle for a moment in the flame. He pushed up the sleeve of his left arm, slowly pushed the needle into his arm above the elbow, emptied the syringe into the muscle. He re-packed the syringe; replaced it with the empty bottle of coramine under the mattress. He put on his torn and dirty jacket; sat on the edge of the bed, his fingers interlocked, looking at the wall in front of him.

He began to think about Eulalia Guimaraes, who seemed such a long way away, such a long time ago. He found difficulty in reconstituting her face in the picture before him. It was only after a moment's thought that he realised that he experienced the difficulty because the face of the new woman—of Tanga—persisted more vibrantly in his memory. He grinned wryly. He thought it strange that at a time like this a man should be concerned with the relative beauty of two women.

But was it strange? Was anything strange? He sat there for what seemed a long time. Now his brain was beginning to clear. The coramine and the injection were beginning to take effect. O'Mara drew a deep breath. He was experiencing the pleasant sensation of power, complete control, co-ordination, that invariably came to him when the coramine began to work. A certain satisfaction based on nothing, dependent on nothing, unlasting but nevertheless satisfying.

Downstairs the telephone began to jangle.

Almost immediately he experienced a reaction; a sudden mental depression that came with the realisation of what the telephone jangle meant. He sat on the bed looking straight before him. Downstairs the telephone continued to ring. There was a lot of time, thought O'Mara. There was no need to hurry; the exchange would go on ringing and ringing until someone answered. It always did. He remembered evenings when both he and Volanon had been too drunk to move; when the telephone had continued to ring with its irritating jangle—a macabre accompaniment to his own alcoholic dreams. He thought: So this will be Taudrille.

He began to think about Taudrille; to wonder what he was like. He shrugged his shoulders; pushed himself up from the bed with his hands; walked across the room, down the dirty wooden uncarpeted stairway to the garage floor. He went across to the ramshackle office in the corner; took the telephone receiver from its cradle.

He said: "Hello, this is the *Garage Volanon* . . . Philippe Garenne."

A voice said: "Monsieur Garenne, my name is Taudrille. Possibly you have heard of me?"

O'Mara said: "Yes. I was told that you would telephone at six o'clock."

Taudrille said: "I am invariably punctual."

O'Mara said: "Yes?"

The voice went on: "The position, Monsieur Garenne, is a little acute at the moment. I think quite soon you will have some visitors. I think already you have some ideas about the gentlemen who will come to see you."

O'Mara said: "Yes, I have some ideas." He leaned against the wooden rickety table. He began to sweat a little.

The voice continued: "I do not believe there is a great deal of necessity for you to worry *too* much. You understand what I mean?"

O'Mara grinned cynically. He said: "Yes, I understand. At the same time it is impossible not to worry a little."

Taudrille said: "But of course. Actually, at the moment, I am forty miles away from you, but I have an excellent car and the road is good. I shall be with you at the latest in three-quarters of an hour. I do not think that our friends will have sufficient time to make themselves too unpleasant."

O'Mara said: "I hope you're right." There was a silence.

The voice said: "Well, *au revoir,* Monsieur Garenne."

O'Mara said: "*Au'voir.*" He hung up the receiver.

He sat on the wooden table, looking straight before him. He thought: *This is it.* He remembered many instances during the war when he had been in tough situations; when things looked

very bad, but he hadn't worried very much in those days. He was
O'Mara then—*the* O'Mara. Now. . . . He held his right hand up
in front of him. It was trembling. He experienced hot and cold
flushes. The pain in his leg had started again.

He grinned. He said to himself: *"Oh, what a fool was there,
my countryman."* He thought that Shakespeare probably had a
decided sense of humour too. Shakespeare, who had something
to say about every possible situation that could conceivably arise
in life.

He got up from the table. He wondered what Shakespeare
would have to say about this one.

After a moment he came out of the little office; crossed the
garage floor; went outside; sat looking across the estuary. It was a
warm evening. The sun was fading. Everything, thought O'Mara,
looked very beautiful. He began to think about the woman Tanga.
Then he began to think about Eulalia Guimaraes. He wondered
why it was that at a time like this the faces of women invariably
obtruded on one's thoughts. After a while he moved over; sat
down on the ground; rested his back against the low white wall.
He sat there waiting.

It was just after six-thirty when the car arrived. It came out
of the narrow main street of the village; came down the estuary road at speed; stopped with a squeal of brakes outside the
garage. The man in the passenger seat opened the door and got
out. He closed the door; stood leaning his back against it, looking
at O'Mara. He was a tall, thin man. His face was of a deep olive
colour. He had a black pencil-line moustache. The man's clothes
were nondescript. He might have been anything. The car was an
Opel that had seen much service.

The driver of the car got out on the other side. He came round
the bonnet. He stood a few feet from the car, looking at O'Mara.
He was about five feet six inches in height; very thin. His jawbones
were high and stood out. Beneath the jawbones the white flesh of
his cheeks caved in. It was as if someone had stretched a pallid
skin on the framework of a skeleton's face. His eyes were narrow.
He wore a cheap ready-made French suit that was too big for him,

with a soft black hat pulled down over one eyes. He looked like an old-time cinema picture of a small-time gangster of the 1935 era in Chicago; but with a difference.

The difference was that the man's face was without hope or expectation. It was dead. The eyes gazed straight out from the thin, pallid face; they did not move; they were without expression and seemed to be fixed like dull headlights. The man stood there, relaxed, his hands hanging straight down by his sides, with the dull and expressionless eyes fixed on O'Mara. He looked like a death's head with an animated body attached—a body that went through certain movements in spite of itself.

The man was without hope or soul or real being. That was what O'Mara thought.

He said: "Good evening, Messieurs. Can I do anything for you?"

The short man said in a very soft voice with a peculiar metallic timbre behind the words: "It seems that there is some trouble with the petrol feed-pipe. At first I thought it was an air bubble. As you know, the quality of the petrol is very bad these days. But now I think there is a stoppage somewhere between the tank and the carburettor; not a complete stoppage—enough petrol will get through for the car to go—but to go badly. You understand?"

O'Mara said: "I understand. It is not an uncommon occurrence these days when cars have been laid up for a long while, although"—he smiled a little—"your car does not look as if it had been laid up."

Neither of the men said anything. O'Mara got up slowly; walked to the car; raised the bonnet on the near side. He looked at the engine of the car. It was in good condition. It had been cleaned recently. He unscrewed the valve connection on the petrol pipe six or seven inches from the carburettor. His fingers seemed to be behaving quite well.

The man who had got out of the passenger seat, who had been leaning against the door, moved away. He looked down the narrow road towards the village. Then he moved near to O'Mara.

He said: "I shouldn't bother yourself with that if I were you."

O'Mara looked down. He saw that the man was holding in his right hand a short Luger pistol. The barrel of the pistol was a few inches from O'Mara's stomach.

He said: "I agree." He smiled. "I will not bother with this. But I think I'd better screw up the connection." He did this. Then he said: "Well?"

The short man said in a dull voice: "Get into the passenger seat. Don't argue or try to do anything stupid; otherwise it will be very bad for you."

O'Mara grinned. For some reason which he could not determine, and in spite of the circumstances, he felt vaguely amused. "Thank you very much," he said. "I suppose I may take it that if I *don't* argue and behave in an unstupid manner, everything will be very good for me?"

The man shrugged his shoulders. He said: "Why should we waste time in futile discussion, Get in."

O'Mara got into the passenger seat. He realised that the pain in his left leg was gone; that he did not feel so bad after all. He thought, and smiled inwardly at the idea, that something had happened to "take him out of himself." The joke appealed to his sense of humour.

The short man with the thin face slipped into the driving seat. The man with the Luger pistol got into the back of the car.

The car turned; drove slowly down the little road, through the village, out on the other side, on to the dirt road that led round the estuary. It accelerated. When it passed the small church and the yew-tree grove it was travelling rapidly.

O'Mara looked out of the window. Across the estuary he could see the *Garage Volanon* illuminated by the fading sun.

The man in the back of the car said: "It is unnecessary for you to look out of the window. You will keep your eyes on the floor of the car."

O'Mara said: "Nuts to you." He said it in English, and then he said it—but rather more strongly—in French.

The man in the back of the car raised his hand and struck a sharp blow on the top of O'Mara's head with the flat of the Luger pistol butt. O'Mara slumped forward. His forehead hit the dashboard. He remained in that position, unconscious, and a little stream of blood began to drip from his cut forehead on to the floor of the car.

The man driving the car looked sideways. He said tonelessly: "These methods seem very coarse and without real artistry. If some stupid member of the *gendarmerie* were to stop the car there would be explanations. Your action was entirely without reason. Having regard to what is going to happen it did not matter one iota whether he saw where we were going or not."

The other shrugged his shoulders. He said: "Possibly. But he does not please me—this one. And it amused me to do that to him."

The car drove on towards the approaching shadows.

The house stood back from the road. It was dilapidated, and, as the car drove up the carriage-drive, which was overgrown with grass and weeds, O'Mara opened his eyes and sat back in the passenger seat.

One side of the house had been hit by a bomb or some form of explosive. The wall had fallen down and lay—a mass of crumpled masonry—half across the carriage-drive. But the right-hand side of the house was merely pock-marked by splinters; the windows were broken and there was an air of unhappy desolation about the place. O'Mara wondered who had lived there and what had happened to them.

The sun had gone and it had begun to rain. The thin-faced man drove carefully round the pile of fallen rubble, past the front of the house, and steered the car round the far side. The drive narrowed to a dirt path. The car stopped at the back of the house before a door set in a recessed porch which was overgrown with ivy.

The man in the back of the car got out. He stood, looking through the front window at O'Mara. After a moment he said: "Get out."

O'Mara got out. He felt very weak, but not at all nervous. He thought, with an inward grin, that he felt better than he had for some time. Life was like that. He ruminated momentarily on the fact that it took a large-sized bunch of trouble to take one's mind off smaller happenings.

He stood a few paces from the door looking at the man with the Luger pistol, who was opening the rusty padlock—with one hand, an eye on O'Mara. The other man drove the car away.

The door swung open. The man with the pistol said: "Go in, and walk straight down the passage in front of you. It's dark, but I'll put on the light when I come to the switch."

O'Mara began to walk down the passage. After a moment he heard a click and surprisingly an electric light was lit.

He said: "I should like to know who you are. I think, in the circumstances, I ought to know your name." He grinned over his shoulder at the man behind him.

The man with the pistol said: "Stop." He opened a door on the left of the passage. He went on: "Go in. You'll find a chair on the other side of the room. And my name is Morosc—but that fact won't be of any help to you."

"Possibly not," said O'Mara. "But it's still very interesting." He walked across the room. The man with the pistol switched on another light. O'Mara saw the chair and sat down. After a moment the man who had driven the car came in. He stood with his back to the door looking at O'Mara.

The room was unfurnished except for two or three chairs. There were no windows. The electric light bulb was dirty, and the room had not been swept for a long time. O'Mara noticed these things automatically and almost subconsciously; because he had been trained to notice things.

His head was aching dully. Now and again he experienced a slight tremor in the stomach. He thought that this was due to the fact that he hadn't had a drink for some time. His insides were not used to such abstinence. He wondered when he would have the next drink.

The man with the pistol came over and stood in front of O'Mara, looking down at him. The sleeve of his coat was short and he wore a wrist-watch on a brown leather strap. O'Mara looked at the watch, which had a peculiarly engraved face, and tried to work out what the time was. After a few moments he came to the conclusion that it was five minutes to seven. He wondered about Taudrille. . . . He remembered vaguely something that the woman Tanga had said about it being not so good if Taudrille was not able to arrive on time. According to the time, this place could not be far from the estuary. O'Mara wondered just where Taudrille was at this moment.

The man who had been leaning against the door came over. They both looked at O'Mara.

There was a silence for a little while. Then the short man said in his oddly stilted French: "It is necessary that you answer certain questions. You may be sure that you will eventually answer them. After you have told us what we wish to know you will be shot. That will happen in any event. But the process will be quick. You will be extremely wise therefore to decide to answer our questions promptly; otherwise we shall find means of making you talk, and my colleague here—when the time comes for shooting—will kill you in such a way that it will take some time for you to die. You understand?"

When the man finished talking he smiled at O'Mara. It was a strange, almost pitiful, smile. It seemed that the thin face was entirely unaccustomed to the process of relaxing; as if the smile was an effort produced after a difficult mental concentration.

O'Mara looked at him. He said a very rude one-syllable word in French. The man with the pistol raised his foot and pushed over the chair on which O'Mara sat. As O'Mara hit the floor the tall man kicked him in the stomach.

O'Mara got up with difficulty. The tall man struck him across the face with the Luger pistol. O'Mara fell sideways, lay against the wall—half lying, half sitting.

The other man said softly: "Not too much at once, Morosc. You are always too eager." He said to O'Mara: "We have been observing you for some time. You are a drunkard and your breaking point is not far off. However, you can still feel enough for our purpose. You will tell me, please, the name and present whereabouts of the person for whom you worked during the war. The person who was responsible for your operations in Lisbon and in South America. Who was that man? What was his name; what does he look like; where is he?"

O'Mara moved so that he could see the man questioning him. He put his hands on the floor and tried to lever himself up. He had no strength. He slumped back against the wall.

He ran his dry tongue over his broken and bleeding lips. He said the rude word once more.

The thin man said in a taut voice: "Go to work, Morosc."

Morosc knelt down beside O'Mara. He picked up one limp arm and placed it under his arm. He clamped the arm between his side and his own arm. The hand and fingers protruded. Then he handed the pistol to the short man, produced a lighter from his coat pocket with his right hand; snapped on the flame; held it between O'Mara's fingers.

A few seconds passed. Then O'Mara made a thin crying noise. Morosc removed the lighter.

The short man said: "Well . . .?"

O'Mara tried to speak. His lips moved but no sound came. The short man put his hand in his pocket and produced a flask. He handed it to Morosc, who still knelt with O'Mara's hand protruding from his armpit.

Morosc put the lighter on the floor; took the flask; put the neck of it into O'Mara's mouth and tilted it.

O'Mara coughed weakly.

The short man said: "Well . . .?"

O'Mara was thinking. But the process was difficult. The white-hot pain was moving from his fingers into his hand and wrist, up his arm. He was thinking that it was necessary that he remembered his conversation with Quayle. If he did that, he would be able not to hurry too much. If he did that . . .

Morosc said in an impatient voice: "Well . . . are you going to speak? Or shall I give you some more?"

O'Mara looked at him with dull eyes. He was thinking of the words Quayle had used. . . . *"You've got to let them think that they've forced it out of you. Don't talk too quickly or they'll smell a rat. They're damned clever . . . too damned clever. You'll have to let them get tough with you before you speak. They know your record. They know you're as tough as hell and, even allowing for the drink and your condition, they'll expect you to put up a show. Just as they'd put up a show. You've got to allow for that."*

With an effort he moved his head nearer to Morosc. Morosc bent forward. O'Mara spat in his face.

The short man began to laugh softly. He said: "Continue, Morosc. He is still very impertinent. He wishes to be brave."

Morosc snapped on the lighter.

Tears began to run down O'Mara's cheeks. His head sagged sideways. A small hissing sound of agony escaped his lips.

The short man said: "Enough, Morosc. I consider that he will talk. Tell him what we shall do to him if he does not talk now. The thing with the nails . . ."

Morosc told O'Mara. He told him with his face almost touching that of the man on the floor. He told O'Mara with a certain whispered satisfaction.

O'Mara began to speak in a soft monotone that was almost a groan. One side of his face was cut and bruised; his lips were smashed. He spoke with difficulty.

He said weakly: "The man was named Quayle. . . . at the International Refrigeration Company in London . . . short and with blue eyes. . . ."

He stopped speaking as the door was kicked open.

The short man who now held the Luger pistol spun round. As he did so the person who had kicked open the door fired from the hip. Morosc coughed and fell on his face. Simultaneously, the short man threw the pistol at the newcomer. It hit the man in the doorway in the face. He jumped to one side. The short man sprang for the doorway; disappeared. The sound of his running footsteps on the bare boards of the passageway could be heard in the room.

The newcomer walked quickly across the room. He stood looking at O'Mara, who regarded him dully.

He said: "I am Taudrille. I regret that for once I am not punctual. It is perhaps unfortunate."

Taudrille drove the car at speed. It was a Delage touring car, with the hood and side-pieces up. The speedometer hovered between the fifty-five and sixty mile an hour indications. O'Mara noted that, although the car was of foreign manufacture, and the number French, the dashboard was of English make. He wondered why.

Taudrille was a compact, good-figured man of somewhere between thirty-five and forty years of age. He radiated an air of cheerful well-being; gave the impression that nothing short of an earthquake could disturb his equanimity. His face was round, the eyes big and brown, set wide apart. The hair showing under the brim of the brown felt hat was curly and dark brown in colour. His hands were peculiar; the fingers short and spatulate. O'Mara observed that the fingers were very short in comparison with the palms and backs of the hands, which were inclined to length. A good workmanlike hand.

An interesting type, this Taudrille. O'Mara wondered where Quayle had found this one. If he *had* found him. Possibly Tanga had discovered Taudrille. One never knew with Quayle. People came and went but they were always carefully selected for the particular job in hand; always *right* for it. Never, thought O'Mara, did Quayle miscast a person for the *role* he intended them to play.

He sat back in the passenger seat and watched Taudrille. Taudrille, he thought, might have been unpunctual earlier in the evening, but he was certainly making up for lost time. And he could drive a car. He sat, hunched over the wheel, after the manner of racing drivers, his eyes on the road, the unlit cigarette stub hanging from the left-hand corner of his mobile mouth.

A practical one—Taudrille. So O'Mara thought. He looked at his injured hand which hung in the sling made out of his necktie. Taudrille had smothered the burned fingers in motor oil from the spare can; covered the hand with two handkerchiefs. O'Mara hoped that the oil was fairly clean.

The hand throbbed maddeningly; the pain was now running up the arm to the shoulder. Beyond that, O'Mara felt fairly well. The cool evening air that came through the vent in the side-piece, and the small flask of not-so-bad brandy that he held in his good hand, were responsible for the temporary feeling of well-being.

Taudrille slowed down for a sharp bend. He said: "I should have gone after him if I had not been certain of my facts and of my man. I know him. He is Nago. He has been working for the Werewolf organisation ever since the Nazis decided that they would no longer exist as a Party. I know all about him. First of all he drugs—but excessively. He drugs and then he drinks. He is not in good shape either mentally or physically. But he has a certain cleverness and a certain occasional mental toughness that is somewhat amazing."

He swivelled the damp cigarette stub to the other corner of his mouth. O'Mara took another swig at the brandy flask.

Taudrille continued: "The time—as you see—is now only a quarter of an hour past seven. Very well. Nago has no car. If I had not spent time smashing the carburettor of his auto I should possibly have been able to arrive a little earlier. But I did what I thought was best. So what can Nago do? All he can do is to make his way to Saint Lys and wait for a train from there. There is no train until eight o'clock, and we shall be there before that time. Nago cannot find any sort of transport between here and Saint Lys unless he asks a passing car or cart for a life. He dare not do that. He must keep off the main roads. Is that not sense?"

O'Mara said: "It sounds reasonable. But he might telephone someone *en route*. He might give the information that they forced out of me to someone from a telephone call-box."

Taudrille was silent whilst he negotiated a curve. Then he accelerated. The Delage shot forward. He said: "No . . . Nago dare not risk a call being checked. Besides that, I tell you that there is no call-box between here and Saint Lys. Nago will keep to the fields and make for Saint Lys. He must do that. Especially if he considered that the information they extracted from you is valuable—as you say it is. He will not risk telephoning that information. Also there is another reason why he would not telephone."

O'Mara asked: "What reason?"

"The man I shot was Morosc," Taudrille answered. "Morosc is known. He is known to the Second Bureau. Nago will certainly think that *I*, at any rate, know of Morosc, and that I would immediately send out an alarm call to pick up Nago. He will imagine that every telephone exchange is waiting for him to get on to a telephone and try to speak to someone; that they will check the call and put a cordon round the district. That is what he will think. And so he will do nothing except make for Saint Lys as quickly as possible on foot. Once he is in a train he will feel safe."

O'Mara said: "I think you are right. How long will it take us?"

"Like this," said Taudrille, "it will take us another twenty minutes."

He took one hand off the wheel; fumbled in his jacket pocket; produced some cigarettes. He held them towards O'Mara. "Light one for me," he said. "And smoke, my friend. There is a lighter in the dashboard. Nothing is so bad when you smoke."

O'Mara lit the cigarettes. He passed one to Taudrille; sat back and relaxed in the passenger seat. He drew the tobacco smoke down into his lungs; thought that when all things were considered the evening might have been worse.

Actually, his reaction to the events since the arrival of the woman Tanga in the afternoon was one of relief. In effect, the things that had happened were good for O'Mara, inasmuch as he had ceased to think about himself, the effects of alcohol, the general depressions of the last months. He was concerned with more important things. He was *working*. He was in effect once more O'Mara.

It was dusk when Taudrille stopped the car outside a small *bistro* on the outskirts of Saint Lys. He lit a fresh cigarette; leaned on the driving wheel; then, suddenly, turned his head towards O'Mara.

"I have a plan," he said. He smiled cheerfully. "I think it will be good if you go into the *bistro*; get yourself a drink and something to eat, and await my return. I shall leave the car here. I shall go to the *depot* and see if I can find our friend. If I find him I shall get him away to some quiet place and finish him."

O'Mara said: "As easily as that?"

Taudrille shrugged his shoulders.

"There should be no great difficulty once I have found him," he said thoughtfully. "Consider that this Nago has been employed by the Nazis first of all and then the Werewolf organisations. But he has never been anything first class—nothing that mattered in a big way. You understand? He has been one of the hewers of wood and drawers of water. Probably this business with you is the first really important thing that he has done. They are forced to employ him because they have not better material to work for them. Their underground *personnel*—as you probably know—is not what it used to be."

O'Mara nodded.

"So," Taudrille went on, "at this moment he is probably feeling elated. He thinks he has pulled something out of the bag—something really big. He may not be of a careless type but he will probably consider that I should spend a certain amount of time, at any rate, in looking after you; in taking you to some place where you could get that hand properly dressed. He will not think that you are tough enough to go right ahead with the job, which—if you will forgive my saying so—I consider to be a definite achievement. In other words, he will think that he will have an hour or perhaps two hours' start—time enough to get here to Saint Lys; to take a train and go to wherever it is he is going. I should think that would be Paris. Everybody always goes to Paris."

Taudrille grinned sideways at O'Mara. "Then there is another thing," he continued. "Nago, as I well know, is a taker of drugs. Remember he has been up against the French before. Both the Resistance and the *Maquis* special units. And the *Maquis* are still very much alive where spies of the war-time and other traitors are concerned. He is, as I have said, a drug addict. He suffers from periodic nervous attacks and is also in fear of his life. It would be on the cards that after the events of this evening, when his colleague Morosc was killed—probably by some of the *Maquis*"—Taudrille grinned at O'Mara—"because that is what people will *think*; he would arrive here and be scared. He would be especially scared if he encountered, *at the depot,* someone whom he knew had belonged to the Resistance, and who had recognised him. It would be on the cards that he *might* consider the easiest way out of the business would be to kill himself. I shall try it . . . *if* I find him."

O'Mara said: "That's all right with me." He got out of the car. "I'll wait until you come back."

Taudrille said: *"Au revoir."* He got out of the car and walked briskly towards the town. He was whistling as he walked.

O'Mara went into the *bistro*. There were only a few people in the place; busily engaged in discussing their own affairs. O'Mara went to the zinc-topped bar at the end of the room. The fat *patron*—his hair slicked down and with an old-fashioned quiff—regarded him with astonishment.

O'Mara shrugged his shoulders. "What would you?" he said. "These damned automobiles. First of all this fool knocks me down—this son of a pig; may he be damned in hell. Then, when I am trying to struggle to my feet, he—concerned, I have no doubt— backs the car and once again runs over the top of my fingers." He ordered a *bock* and two *croissants*.

The *patron* said: "That is how things go. You are lucky to be alive. You should receive a great deal of compensation. Your face is no longer very attractive."

O'Mara presented an extraordinary sight. One side of his face was terribly bruised and discoloured from the bridge of the nose to the chin. The skin had begun to turn a brownish hue under his eyes. Both his lips were split, and there was a jagged tear—caused by the safety catch of Morosc's pistol—down one cheek.

He put the *croissants* in his right-hand pocket; picked up the drink; went to a table in the corner.

He rested his injured hand on the table; took out the *croissants*; began to eat. His mouth was dry and his burned fingers were very painful. He hoped that he would not lose the fingernails. He hoped that would not happen, not because he minded the pain, but because it would be inconvenient and, at the moment, he disliked the idea of being inconvenienced. He thought on these lines because, in spite of everything, he felt in fairly good shape, and there was a great deal for him to do.

O'Mara was not unhappy. He was a man who was essentially practical, and with that practicality was mixed an inspired spark of genius for his own particular work that had made him Quayle's most outstanding agent during the war years. To O'Mara, sitting at the table in the small *bistro*, the events of the last six months—

of this afternoon and evening—were merely so many moves in a game which, so far as he was concerned, had merely started. . . .

Whatever Quayle might think.

He thought about Quayle. Quayle would probably consider—if he had known of the events of the evening—that O'Mara would lay off. He would consider himself entitled to think that O'Mara would have had enough to go on with; that he would be glad of a rest. Perhaps he thought that. Or did he? Perhaps he didn't!

O'Mara grinned, finished the *bock,* carried the glass to the bar, ordered another. He told a funny story to the *patron* and returned to his table.

He sat there, eating and drinking; occasionally looking out of the small window behind him, watching the dusk falling, wondering about Taudrille.

It seemed to O'Mara that a long time had gone by. There was no clock on the wall of the *bistro*; he had no watch and he was disinclined to ask the *patron.* He concluded that at the moment time was not of great importance.

He began to think about the woman Tanga. He decided to think about her. The process enabled him to forget the pain in his hand; his tiredness; his general *malaise.* He tried to remember things about her.

He had met her once—in the Argentine. But he had known then that she was working for Quayle; that she was considered to be a first-class operative and that she had been in one or two very tough spots and got out of them with good technique and a certain amount of the glamour which sometimes accompanies such events.

He remembered her. It had been in Rio, and O'Mara, working with Michael Kells, had been interested in a man named Pasquale Punta—a man of *aliases* and quite a few languages. Punta had strutted for a time on the stage and then disappeared in a back street one night, to be found a week later on a refuse heap outside the city limits. A not uncommon occurrence in those days.

Tanga had been with a man—one Senhor Eivada Intaces; an important person who was supposed to be hand in glove with Hitler's top agents in that part of the world. O'Mara had gone to a party—he was on some job or other in connection with the Punta business—and Tanga had been receiving. She was acting as hostess for Intaces.

O'Mara knew who she was; what she was doing; and as he shook hands with her had given her a quick appraising glance; had tried to come to some conclusion about her.

He had failed. He remembered now that he had summed her up as an elusive type. Beautiful but elusive and remote. He thought that now, possibly, he might be able to find out a little more about her. Not that it really mattered.

He began to think about the man Morosc and the thin-faced Nago. . . .

He felt very tired.

It was just after nine o'clock when Taudrille came into the *bistro*. An unsmoked cigarette stub hung from the left-hand corner of his mouth. O'Mara thought that he was probably thinking about something; that when he concentrated he forgot to light or relight his cigarettes. He wondered what Taudrille would be thinking about.

His left hand was hurting abominably. The pain had settled down to a steady pulsating nag. The area of the pain covered the whole of his hand and wrist and some of the arm. He wondered how long it would take for the fingers to heal; how soon he could get someone to look at the injury. The idea of sepsis did not appeal to him. He needed his hands too much to be playing about with doctors for weeks—if not longer. He swore under his breath.

Taudrille came over and sat down on the seat opposite O'Mara. He was sweating a little. You had to look to notice it, but there was an obvious dampness about his forehead. But his expression denoted satisfaction.

O'Mara said: "Well . . . what about a drink?"

"In a minute," said Taudrille. "First . . . how is the hand? Is it *very* bad?"

"I've known worse things," said O'Mara with a wry smile. "Did you see the boy friend?"

Taudrille laughed softly. There was a quality of cynical amusement about the laugh which came from somewhere in the region of the throat. He took the dead cigarette stub from his mouth and pinched it between his forefinger and thumb. He threw the stub on the floor and trod on it.

"The boy friend," he said very quietly. "Like that . . ." He looked at the trodden cigarette end.

O'Mara said: "Good. What goes on?"

Taudrille grinned at O'Mara; got up; went to the bar. He ordered *vermouth cassis* in a loud and cheerful voice; came back with the drink in his hand. He sat down.

"It was just as I thought," he said. "It was just like that, only it was a little more sad—a little pitiful. If you understand me. That Nago . . ." Taudrille shrugged his shoulders; picked up the *vermouth cassis*; drank it in one comprehensive gulp.

"Go on," said O'Mara. "You do like a spot of dramatics, don't you?" There was a touch of admiration in his voice.

Taudrille laughed. He nodded. "I like to paint the complete picture," he said. "Actually, I am rather pleased with events since I left you here. It was as I thought. I went straight to the *depot*. There is a little waiting-room—a ramshackle affair—at the end of the platform, and there was a train for Paris at twelve minutes past eight."

O'Mara asked: "He was there?"

"He was there," repeated Taudrille. "He was sitting on the bench, huddled up against the wall in the corner. He looked very depressed and rather ill. There was no one else in the waiting-room."

O'Mara grinned. "He must have liked that," he said.

"He didn't like it—not at all," said Taudrille. "When I went in and showed him the pistol, he looked at me with the eyes of a dog that is about to have its throat cut. But with a certain hopelessness which seemed to indicate that the throat-cutting would not matter so very much after all."

"I expect he was tired," said O'Mara.

Taudrille nodded. "That—and also I think he needed some drug. I imagine that it is some time, possibly a day or so, since he had whatever it is he took, and he was feeling that too. I talked to him. I talked to him like a father."

O'Mara grinned again. He thought Taudrille was pretty good.

"I told him that he hadn't a dog's chance. I told him that in any event he was finished, and that it would be good for him to make it as easy for himself as he could. I said that I could do one of two things. I pointed out to him something that he knew very well; that the *Maquis* groups around Saint Lys, Gouarec, and Pont Laroche, were still very active; still pulling in war-time traitors and Nazi adherents. I told him that if I handed him over to the *Maquis* he would have a damned bad time and that there would be precious little left of him by the time they'd finished with him. On the other hand I said that if he liked to confide in me I would listen to what he cared to say and then hand him over to the local police, who would see that he was sent off to the Second Bureau for interrogation. I said that if he played his cards well with the Second Bureau, and liked to make himself agreeable, they would probably be prepared to use him in order to contact the people for whom he was working. That he might continue to live."

O'Mara asked: "How did he like that?"

"He liked it," said Taudrille. "He told me as much as he could, but of course he is only very small fry and did not know anything of value. He had been working with Morosc, who was a Suedeten German, and he knew no one except Morosc and one other nondescript individual whom he described but whose name he did not know. They had been waiting for a long time to get at you. They knew about you. They knew that you had worked for the Anglo-French 'B' Syndicate on *contre-espionage* during the war, and that you had done a lot against the Germans in Lisbon and the Argentine. They knew you were an important *agent*. Somebody had been tailing you ever since you were in Paris, and when you arrived at Saint-Brieuc, their orders were to strike immediately you were ripe for it. They thought you'd left the Service and were trying to drink yourself into forgetfulness—which is a thing that many *agents* have tried to do "—Taudrille smiled amiably—"not always successfully."

O'Mara said: "Then what?"

"I took him away from the waiting-room. He thought I was going to hand him over to the Saint Lys *gendarmerie*. He seemed a little more hopeful. Also I bought him a double glass of extremely bad brandy at a *bistro,* which he liked very much. I took from him a ridiculous little .25 Mauser pistolet—one of those things that Himmler used to give to the lady members of his External Units to carry in their handbags."

O'Mara yawned. He was very tired.

Taudrille went on: "I said we would take a shortcut to the *gendarmerie* place. We went across the path that goes over the fields behind the Saint Lys *depot.* There is a little wood there. I took him through the wood, and when we were well out of sight I talked to him again. We sat under a tree and had a little talk. I told him that I was going to shoot him in any event, and that if he liked to do what I wanted I would see that he died very quickly. I also told him *where* I would shoot him if he *didn't* do what I wanted."

O'Mara said: "Ah. . . . He must have liked that a lot too."

"Eventually he did what I wanted," said Taudrille casually. "He wrote a suicide note. He signed it. When he had done that I gave him a cigarette, and whilst he was lighting it I put the barrel of the ridiculous little .25 Mauser in his ear and blew out whatever he used to consider were his brains. Then I cleaned the pistol butt and put it in his hand. And that was the end of that."

O'Mara sighed. There was a certain satisfaction in the sigh. He said: "What did he say in the note?"

Taudrille said with a smile: "I think of everything. I made a copy for you." He produced a piece of paper; handed it across the table.

O'Mara took it. He read:

"I have had enough. My name is known as one who worked against France and the Allies. Sooner or later the Maquis or someone else will get me. I am tired and desire to die."

O'Mara said: "Excellent. That ought to tie the ends up. Let's get out of here."

He put the piece of paper in his pocket.

Taudrille got up. He said: "I am at your disposal. I await your instructions. Possibly you are aware of what is to happen now?"

O'Mara said: "I haven't an idea. But something or somebody will turn up. It always does. My own people will be waiting to act somehow or other. I'll have to find out."

Taudrille said: "Paris?"

"No," O'Mara answered. "I want to go back to Saint-Brieuc. But I mustn't be seen around the place. I've got to lie low. That won't be difficult because I've friends there. . . ."

"Excellent," said Taudrille. "I am a great admirer of your English organisations. They are always very good."

O'Mara grinned ruefully. He looked at his bandaged hand. "They've been bloody good to me," he said. He drew on his cigarette. He got up from his seat.

"You'd better run me back to Saint-Brieuc," he said. "On the far side of the estuary. There's a little church up there and a yew-tree grove. You can drop me off near there and I'll show you where you can contact my friends. I daren't risk going into Saint-Brieuc—even in the car. I'll stay up there in the yew-tree grove. After you've seen my people you can come back, pick me up and get me off somewhere or other out of the district where I can get this hand seen to."

Taudrille said: "Excellent."

They nodded to the *patron*; went out; got into the car. Taudrille started the engine. He said as he let in the clutch: "Not a bad day. You will forgive me if I tell you that I consider you to be an extremely brave man."

O'Mara grinned. He reached for the brandy flask in the dashboard pocket.

He settled back in the passenger seat; closed his eyes.

The clock on the dashboard showed that it was a quarter-past ten. Taudrille stopped the car in the shadow of the yew-tree grove by the little church on the far side of the estuary.

He looked at O'Mara, who was sitting in the passenger seat with his eyes closed. For a moment Taudrille thought he was asleep.

O'Mara opened his eyes.

"Drive off the road on to that grass verge in the shadow," he said. "Then we can cut through the churchyard and on to the cliff path."

Taudrille did as O'Mara said. They got out of the car. O'Mara led the way through the yew-tree grove and skirted the low wall of the churchyard; the wall over which he had stumbled not very long ago.

It was a beautiful night. The moon was full and its radiance glittered on the waters of the estuary, reaching out to the sea, like a long silver streak.

Life, thought O'Mara, was damned funny. In London, in Paris, in all sorts of places, people would be drinking their after-dinner liqueurs; or sitting in theatres. Men would be talking in clubs in St. James's Street. People would be recalling days of the war; congratulating themselves that it was over; remembering the "doodle-bugs" and the bombs.

Young officers, just demobilised, would be saying good-bye to all *that*—some of them regretfully.

Good-bye to all *what*? O'Mara grinned sardonically at the thought. Good-bye to goddam nothing. With a world that was still sizzling, and the word already going round that the Japanese secret societies were already getting organised for the time when revenge might be possible.

He mentally shrugged his shoulders.

They came out on to the cliff path. The path wound, like a narrow ribbon, along the cliff edge; broadened into the dirt road that ran round the estuary and presently ran into the fishing village. It was on this path that O'Mara had stumbled this morning. He remembered his impression, his anger at the thought of returning to the garage; of seeing Volanon; of continuing his dreary existence.

So much had happened since then.

Behind him, Taudrille was humming a tune very softly. O'Mara stopped and Taudrille came up to his side. O'Mara pointed across the estuary.

"Straight across," he said, "you can see a white wall—the one right in the moonlight. Got it? Well, just to the left is a white building. That is the *Garage Volanon*. Alongside the garage you can see a light. That will be the window of the *Café Volanon*. Both those places are on the estuary road."

Taudrille nodded. O'Mara moved forward. He stood on the cliff edge looking for another landmark.

"Follow the road until it reaches the edge of the houses," he said. "That is the beginning of the main road. It runs through the town. You just get on to that road and follow it. Now listen carefully and impress what I am going to tell you on your mind."

Taudrille said: "I am concentrating very carefully."

"There is a villa called *Cote d'Azur,*" O'Mara went on. "You will drive along the main road out of the town and you will come to a group of three trees on the left of the road. The trees are about a mile and a half out of the town. A mile past the trees is a dirt road leading off to the left. Turn down that road. It looks as if it is too narrow for a car but after a bit it widens out."

Taudrille said: "I understand. The estuary road from the *Garage* and *Café Volanon*; through the town for a mile and a half. Three trees on the left and the first left turn."

"Right," said O'Mara. "You drive along the dirt road for half a mile and then you find a white gate on your right. The name of the Villa is on the gate—*Cote d'Azur.* You will go in and you will ask for Madame. You will meet a lady. You will give her this message."

O'Mara looked about him; then drew near to Taudrille. He put his face close to Taudrille's ear. He said: "You will tell her this from O'Mara . . ."

He stepped back quickly; put his foot in the middle of Taudrille's back; kicked forward with every ounce of strength that he possessed.

Taudrille went over the cliff edge. O'Mara heard the sound of his body hitting a crag and the dull thud as it hit the rocks at the bottom.

He stood there, sweating with the expenditure of strength that had been necessary to remove Taudrille from this life. Taudrille, he thought, must have been very much surprised—too surprised to shout. O'Mara wondered what Taudrille had thought during the few flying seconds before he hit the rocks. He surmised that— if coherent thought had been possible—the dead man must have been inclined—very quickly — to change his opinion as to the stupidity, or otherwise, of O'Mara.

He stepped back and took a loose cigarette from his pocket—one of the cigarettes that Taudrille had given him. He lit it with the lighter that he had taken from the car dashboard.

He covered the flame of the lighter, and then the glowing end of the cigarette, with his right hand. He stood on the edge of the cliff looking over the estuary.

He stood there for a few minutes smoking silently; drawing the tobacco smoke into his lungs; enjoying it.

He threw the cigarette away; stamped it out; kicked it over the cliff edge. He began to walk slowly towards the spot where the cliff face was broken; where he knew he could climb down and inspect what remained of the late Taudrille.

He was very tired. A blister had arrived on his left foot; and his broken lips smarted in the night air. He kept on at a steady slow pace because that was the only way to do it.

It took him a long time to get down to the rocks at the foot of the high cliff. He worked his way over the uneven surfaces of the rocks, moving carefully. He realised that one fall might use up his remaining strength.

It was a good half-hour before he arrived at the spot where Taudrille had crashed.

The body looked like a half-filled sack.

O'Mara stood looking at it for a little while. Then he fumbled in his pocket; found the piece of paper that Taudrille had given him in the Saint Lys *bistro*—the copy of the Nago suicide note. He read it again:

"I have had enough. My name is known as one who worked against France and the Allies. Sooner or later the Maquis or someone else will get me. I am tired, and desire to die."

O'Mara thought that it had been very thoughtful of the late Taudrille to copy the note.

He moved forward. He opened the split, blood-splashed jacket; slipped the note into the top waistcoat pocket; replaced the jacket.

He turned away; began to walk slowly over the rocks, back to the broken path in the cliff face. He was without strength. He moved forward, like an automaton, motivated by a supreme will-power.

It was necessary that he reached the *Villa Cote d Azur* before daylight. It was a long time until daylight, but he had a long way to go. Once on the cliff top he must turn away from Saint-Brieuc; must work right round the outskirts of the town; must approach the Villa from the far side.

That would be fifteen miles, and he must do it in six hours before daylight.

Half-way tip the cliff path he fell. He fell and lay for some minutes before he was able to rise. His mouth had begun to bleed once more. He felt like death.

He rested for a little while at the cliff top. Then he began to make his way slowly along the path, past the churchyard and the yew-tree grove. He was better on the level ground.

It was half an hour later when he came on the house; recognised the bomb-scarred walls and windows; the pile of rubble on the drive. He went through the iron gates, up the drive. At the back, in an open shed at the end of what once had been a flower garden, he found Nago's car. He opened the bonnet, examined the engine. He searched his pockets for a cigarette; discovered that he had none; went back to the road. He began to walk slowly in the direction of Pont Laroche. He intended to give Saint-Brieuc the widest possible berth.

His foot was paining him. He was limping. His left arm—from fingers to shoulder—was burning with pain. Sweat stood out on his forehead.

He began to think about Quayle. He wondered what Quayle was doing—thinking.

Quayle, he thought, would know in his heart that he, O'Mara, would make it—somehow!

Goddam it, he *had* made it!

At a quarter-past five, when the dawn mist was beginning to fade, O'Mara stumbled up the flagged path that led from the rear gate of the *Villa Cote d'Azur*.

He fell heavily against the porch; fumbled for the bell-push; found it; kept his finger on it.

After a while the door opened. Through what seemed to his worn and exhausted eyes to be a thick fog, O'Mara could discern the figure of Tanga as she stood in the doorway. She moved to one side. He could see her lips moving, but he heard nothing.

With a great effort he pushed himself away from the stone porch. He half moved, half stumbled towards the door. He lurched past her; fell on his face in the hallway; struggled; turned over on his back.

She shut the door quietly. She moved quickly to the foot of the stairs at the rear of the wide hall.

She called: "Yvette . . ."

She went back to O'Mara. She stood looking down at him.

One side of his face was an immense bruise. His lips were cut and bleeding. The sole of one broken shoe was missing; the bare foot showing was cut, bleeding and filthy. The bandage on the burned hand was gone, and the fingers—discoloured, covered with the thick motor oil—were not an attractive sight.

She knelt down by him. She said softly: "My drunken O'Mara . . . you are quite superb . . . be patient for a moment. . . ."

The maid appeared. She stood, half-way down the stairs, regarding the scene with interest. She saw O'Mara on the floor.

She said: *"Mon Dieu!"*

Tanga said: "Yvette . . . the brandy quickly. That first . . . then the medical case. Be quick."

Yvette disappeared.

O'Mara opened one eye; then the other. He looked at Tanga. Then, deliberately, and with great mental concentration, he winked at her.

His eyes closed.

She leaned over him; pushed back the stained sleeve and dirty shirt cuff. Her long, white fingers seemed incongruous on his dirty wrist as she counted his pulse.

Yvette appeared in the hall from the side door.

Tanga said: "Yvette . . . give me the hypodermic syringe and the morphia . . ."

O'Mara opened his eyes and looked at her.

She said: "I think a little sleep for you, my friend. At the moment it would seem indicated."

She took the scissors from the first-aid case; slit the coat and shirt sleeves; dabbed surgical spirit above the elbow; deftly injected the morphia.

She stood up; handed the syringe to the maid.

The door-bell rang. The sound of the bell seemed very loud in the hall.

Tanga caught her silk gown about her. She went to the door; opened it. Ernest Guelvada, an airplane bag in his hand, stood on the step.

He smiled at her. His eyes went past her to the maid Yvette; then to the figure of O'Mara, who was, by now, entirely disinterested in everything.

Guelvada said: "Madame la Comtesse de Sarieux? I am Ernest Guelvada—at your service. It would seem that I arrive at an opportune moment."

She said: "Come in. I am glad to meet you."

Guelvada came into the hall. He closed the door quietly. He looked from Tanga to the maid; saw the medical case, the syringe, the morphia bottle. He cast a quick glance at O'Mara.

He put his baggage and his hat on a chair. His face was illuminated by a smile which embraced everything.

He said: "It seems that an interesting time has been had by all. It appears that hostilities have commenced. Perhaps someone will indicate where this distinguished Irishman is to sleep." He pointed to O'Mara.

Yvette moved to the stairs. Guelvada slipped off his coat; leaned over O'Mara. With a double movement, an expert fireman's lift and a supreme effort of strength, he pulled the prone figure over his shoulder.

He raised himself; walked to the foot of the stairs; looked back. He carried the fourteen-stone O'Mara with ease.

He smiled wickedly. He said: "Hostilities have begun. It must not be forgotten that Guelvada is equivalent to an Army Corps. I have no doubt that I shall extract retribution."

He began to climb up the stairs.

She watched him until he disappeared round the bend in the stairway. Then she went to the small table at the side of the hall; found a cigarette; lit it. She picked up the medical case; ascended the stairs.

In front of her, nearing the landing, she could hear Guelvada humming a Belgian love-song.

CHAPTER THREE
ERNESTINE

O'MARA came out of a drugged sleep; opened an eye; ran a parched tongue over dry lips. He watched the shadows on the white carpet. He saw Tanga.

She said: "This is the day after—the *evening* after—the night before. You have slept like an exhausted bear."

O'Mara thought that her accent was charming.

She moved from the bedside, across to the windows that looked down the hill, and out to the sea. She drew on the curtain cord, closed the pale green curtains. She switched on the light; flooded the room with the soft glow from the shaded wall lamps.

The bedroom was long with big windows on the estuary side. The walls and ceilings were painted white; they glowed warmly under the electric lights. The curtains and the bed coverlet were of pale green organdie with white spots. The carpet was thick white pile with green rugs here and there.

In the low wide bed, supported by the green linen pillows, O'Mara bulked incongruously. He filled the bed; appeared strangely to overflow it. A cradle kept the weight of the bedclothes from his injured foot. His left shoulder and arm, protruding from a scarlet silk pyjama jacket borrowed from Guelvada, were bandaged. The arm was in a sling. One side of his face was covered with a lint pad secured by adhesive tape, and, on the other, one eye and half a mouth conveyed an impression of mischievous disdain; near boredom.

She came back to him; stood by the side of the bed, looking at him.

O'Mara regarded her with his single eye. She was dressed in a red silk frock patterned with a floral design in white. She wore white suede sandals, and her dark hair was bound with a red ribbon.

She said: "You present the strangest sight. At this moment you look rather like a bad-tempered porpoise who has, by some unknown means, got himself into my bed. The eye which I can see is slightly bloodshot and entirely malevolent. At the same time I think you should be well satisfied. You are not even dead. . . . Guelvada arrived last night," she concluded.

O'Mara grunted.

She went to the medicine table in the corner of the bedroom; filled a feeding-cup with brandy and soda; brought it to him. She sat on the bed and inserted the spout of the feeding-cup into the corner of his mouth. O'Mara gulped vigorously. She replaced the feeding-cup on the table; returned to the bedside; regarded him with amused eyes.

"I remember you in Rio," she said. "That time when you and one other were chasing that Punta man. You remember, of course. You came to a reception; I was acting as hostess for Intaces, who was then being paid a great deal of money by the Nazis. That was the Intaces who was eventually shot by Michael Kells. Kells had told me about you; had told me of your exploits, and I was looking forward to meeting you. I wanted, so badly, to get a sight of the famous Shaun Aloysius O'Mara. I imagined that you would look like a large and extremely handsome bull. Then I saw you. I was shattered. Absolutely and entirely shattered, because you looked *just* like a large and extremely handsome bull. I had of course hoped that you would look different from what I had thought of you. I had hoped that you would be slim, and handsome, in a dark and somewhat sinister manner; that you would look at me with eyes that were filled with a wicked and predatory light."

She shook her head sadly. She sighed.

"All this . . . years ago," she said. "And now you are lying in my bed, looking exactly as if you had been run over by a motor bus in the Strand in London."

O'Mara said, out of the corner of his mouth: "All right . . . make the most of your time whilst I'm tied here by one leg. One day . . . and not so long to wait either . . . I shall be up and doing, and then . . ."

She said coolly: "Oh, dear . . . how terrified I shall be then."

O'Mara grinned at her. He said: "Ride me as much as you like. But I'd like to tell you something. When I was sitting down there on the estuary, leaning against the wall, and saw your car arrive, it was like a message from heaven. *That* was good. When you got out of the car it was even *better.* I thought you were the loveliest thing I'd ever seen in my life. You were like a breath of oxygen to a bad pneumonia case. I felt that life might even be worth living in spite of everything. . . ."

"Flatterer . . ." she murmured.

O'Mara's eye shone wickedly. "Of course," he went on, "I couldn't realise then that everything is a matter of comparison. The fact that I was dazzled by what *seemed* to be a marvellous figure, a divine walk, a supreme loveliness, means nothing now. Now . . . when I can lie back and remember some of the *really* marvellous women I met in Rio, I can, thank goodness, place you in the right box in my mind. . . ."

"What box?" she asked sharply.

O'Mara stretched. "Quite obviously you are a nice kind, and what I might call homely and comfortable woman," he said, grinning happily. "Is there any more brandy?"

She went to the table and filled the feeding-cup. She shrugged her slim shoulders.

She said: "My God . . . homely . . . and *comfortable*!"

The telephone rang. She went out of the room. He heard her laughing.

A minute passed. Then the buzzer on the bed-table sounded. O'Mara reached for the telephone.

Quayle said: "Hello, Shaun. It's all right. You can talk. This is a cut-out line. Tanga tells me that you're still all in one piece; that they've been tough with you, but that you're still O'Mara. I *thought* you'd get through."

"Nice of you," said O'Mara. "Damned nice. I must say I was extremely glad when Taudrille arrived. They were just going to start on my fingernails . . ."

Quayle said: "Too bad. . . . By the way, what did you think of Taudrille?"

O'Mara said: "Not much. I pushed him over a cliff. Do you like that?"

"Yes," said Quayle. "I thought something like that might happen. Has Guelvada arrived?"

"He came last night," said O'Mara. "He's here now."

Quayle asked seriously: "Can you go on?"

O'Mara muttered darkly into the telephone; "What's all this bloody 'can' stuff? Have you ever known me *not* able to handle something. My face is knocked about and one hand and foot are out of action for a few days; otherwise I'm all right. The thing was good for me. By the way, who knew about this Taudrille? Where did he come from?"

"Epps produced him," said Quayle. "Epps was a near-Nazi who came over to us in the early days whilst the war was still on. Epps talked to save his own skin. I believe they knew about that. Just when the war was ending they slung Taudrille—who was a dyed-in-the-wool Nazi and a Himmler-trained external and internal agent—into a Concentration Camp, and he put up the front that he was a French agent who'd been picked up by the Germans. Epps believed this, and I let him go on believing it. I wanted to see what Taudrille would eventually do. I knew he'd get up to something."

"I see," said O'Mara. "Where do we go from there?"

Quayle said: "You got Taudrille out in to the open. There must be a line from him. I can't be of much help to you at the moment. Have you *any* line—no matter how vague—to work on?"

"Definitely," said O'Mara. "It's sticking out like a pier into the sea. I can go on."

Quayle asked: "What do you want? Guelvada has money and a credit for as much as you may require. Tanga is good for anything you ask her. She's a lovely person, isn't she, Shaun? And clever."

O'Mara said: "I don't know about being clever. She's homely . . . and comfortable. . . . "

Quayle laughed. He said: "I should tell *her* that."

O'Mara grinned. "I *have*," he said. He went on: "I want a contact with the Second Bureau. Give me a Paris contact for research and records and one for local leg work. Ask them to give me a really good contact here, or somewhere near here, with a local *Maquis* group leader or a good Resistance man. I don't care who he is so long as he's absolutely *right*. I only want to use him for support if necessary. Can you do that?"

Quayle said: "It's done. I'll telephone through in an hour with the names."

O'Mara said: "All right."

"You've done a hell of a job," said Quayle. "Are you sure you're all right?"

"Don't be foolish," said O'Mara. "Surely you don't think those bastards could do anything to *me* that could really annoy me?"

"No," said Quayle thoughtfully. "I didn't think they could."

O'Mara asked softly: "Peter . . . where the hell did you find this Tanga? I've never seen anything like her."

He began to cough into the telephone as she came into the room.

Quayle said; "So she's come back. Well . . . don't lose her. She's valuable—as you'll find out. Good luck, Shaun."

"And to you," said O'Mara. He hung up. He said: "A little more brandy, please. Then get that Guelvada one here; gather round me, and listen."

She fetched the brandy. She said: "You ought not to drink any more to-night. You need sleep. I may be homely, but I'm a very good nurse."

O'Mara grinned at her. He said: "It's very funny, but a woman would rather be called ugly than homely." He looked at her keenly with his single eye. He went on: "Actually, you've got something—I *think*. One day I'll get around to telling you about it—when I've time. Now get Guelvada."

She said with a smile: "Of course. I live to serve you." She went out of the room.

O'Mara threw off the bedclothes; swung his legs out of the bed; sat regarding his bandaged foot with interest. He got up; stood on one foot; put the other foot gingerly on the floor; tried to walk. After a few minutes he gave it up; went back to bed.

Tanga and Guelvada came into the room. Guelvada wore a well-cut tuxedo, a silk shirt and collar, a watered silk black tie. O'Mara thought he looked very dressy.

Guelvada brought two chairs to the bedside. He said, as he placed one for Tanga: "Congratulations, O'Mara. I think you have made a splendid recovery. I felicitate you."

O'Mara said: "We'll felicitate each other when we've got this job finished. I'm tied by the leg for a few days, but there's quite a lot can be done. Has anyone a cigarette?"

Guelvada produced cigarettes. He lit them. For a few moments there was silence.

Then: "One of two things are quite obvious," said O'Mara. "I'll tell you what they are. This Taudrille is—or rather was—a Nazi agent. A fairly good and tough specimen, I should say. Quayle had a line on that and wanted to see what Taudrille would get up to. Quayle obviously had an idea that there was a connection between the killing of the *agents* we've lost in the Gouarec district and this Taudrille fellow, but he probably couldn't check on it. He used me to find out."

O'Mara grinned. "I think I've found out," he said.

"Tanga here was the contact with Epps in Paris," he went on. "Epps is probably all right, but a fool. He accepted Taudrille at his face value. He did this because Taudrille had been released from a Nazi Concentration Camp where he'd been specially put in—you know, the old stuff—and because Taudrille had probably told him a good yarn about working for the French Resistance or something like that. In any event, Epps couldn't check, so he chanced it. Understood?"

"Understood," said Guelvada. Tanga nodded.

"Quayle played it the hard way," O'Mara went on. "He put me in here as Philippe Garenne—a no-good drunk—knowing damned well that the Nazis knew who I was. He waited to see what would happen. I came here and started working for Volanon, drinking rot-gut and going from bad to worse. But it came off. Somebody decided that they would have a go to make me talk and find out who the boss was. Epps discovered that. He discovered it and got it to Quayle through Tanga here. Right?"

She nodded. "I am most annoyed," she said. "I believed in Epps. Quayle told me to."

O'Mara laughed. "You ought to know that Quayle never lets even his left hand know what his *left* hand is doing," he said. "Quite obviously, Epps got his information from Taudrille. Now he begins to trust Taudrille. And why not? Doesn't this Taudrille come along and tell him that he has discovered that two Nazi agents—one a certain Morosc, the other a person called Nago—are planning to arrive at Saint-Brieuc and make the supposed Philippe Garenne—whom they know to be O'Mara—talk? Doesn't he do that? Of course he does, and the stupid Epps trusts him."

O'Mara inhaled cigarette smoke.

"Taudrille tells Epps not to worry *too* much. Because he, Taudrille, is going to keep a close eye on these two, and when they arrive in Saint-Brieuc to set about the supposed Garenne, he, Taudrille, will arrive and keep the party nice and clean and wipe up Morosc and Nago in a very big way. Epps reports this to Tanga, who reports it to Quayle. Right?"

"That is quite correct," said Tanga.

"Very well," O'Mara went on. "Quayle is quite happy. Because now he knows that, in some way or another, Taudrille will show his hand. He instructs Tanga to come here and warn me that the time is approaching; that the boys are after me and that Taudrille will telephone me. And now everything is laid on."

O'Mara stubbed out his cigarette in the ash-tray. He thought that he felt very tired.

"Taudrille telephoned me as arranged. But he was in a tough position. He had to tell lies because of what he wanted to do. He told me first of all that he would arrive in time to stop Morosc and Nago getting *too* tough with me. He didn't. He made an excuse about that when he *did* arrive. He told me that he had spent some of the time smashing the carburettor of Nago's car so that he couldn't drive it away. That was a lie. The carburettor wasn't smashed. I examined it. It hadn't been touched.

"When he did arrive he was so obvious that he positively *creaked*. He came in just when the Morosc person was getting really funny with me. He shot Morosc, but he allowed Nago to get away. . . ."

"Ha," said Guelvada. "The old game. Nago was to get away with the information."

"Right," said O'Mara. "Taudrille—or whatever his name really was—let Nago get away. He thought that I was too concerned with my own aches and pains for my brain to be working in top gear. I suggested to him that Nago might pass on the information to someone else. But he rebutted that. He assured me that Nago wouldn't use a telephone; that he couldn't possibly get a lift to Saint Lys; that he would have to walk across country and that we should arrive first. Taudrille *had* to play it that way. He *had* to allow Nago to get to the railway *depot* at Saint Lys where he, Taudrille, *had made an appointment to meet him,* so that Nago could pass over the information he thought he had forced out of me."

"Precisely," said Guelvada with a little smile. "After which our Monsieur Taudrille deals with the unfortunate Nago?"

"Right," said O'Mara. "When we arrived at Saint Lys I was feeling pretty well done in. That was very good for Taudrille. He parked me in a *bistro* and went off, apparently to search for Nago. He returned and informed me that he had found him and killed him. What he does not tell me is that he, Taudrille, was the instigator of the whole scheme and that he has now got rid of both Morosc and Nago, both of whom knew the information which had been extracted from me; and that he is now possibly the only person who is in possession of that information."

O'Mara held out his hand for another cigarette. When it was lit, he said: "If the fool had only told me, when he returned to me at the *bistro,* that he had found Nago at the *depot,* and that Nago had said he had been lucky enough to secure a lift in a car to Saint Lys, there might have been a chance of my believing in him. But when he returned with no explanation as to how Nago had got to Saint Lys in time, I knew that he was in it up to his neck. I saw the whole thing. . . ."

"And then . . .?" asked Tanga.

"We came back," said O'Mara. "We came back to Saint-Brieuc; to the other side of the estuary. We parked the car and went to the cliff edge, so that I could give him directions as to how to get here to the Villa. I pushed him over the edge."

"But delightful," said Guelvada. "A most adequate process. I take it, it is a very long drop?"

"A hell of a drop," said O'Mara. "Then I climbed down the cliff path; found what was left of him and planted a suicide note that he had copied from a note he had left on Nago, whom he had shot in a wood some way behind the Saint Lys *depot*. And that's that."

Guelvada said: "So at this moment the too-enterprising Taudrille is lying at the foot of the cliff somewhere on the other side of the estuary?"

O'Mara nodded. "Something has to be done about that," he said. "I do not think that the body will have been discovered by now. It is in a lonely spot—on the rocks. If it has been found the suicide note will also be found and the explanation *may* be accepted. Anyhow, no one is going to worry a great deal about one unknown more or less in these go-ahead days. But I hope it hasn't been found. I have other ideas."

"Yes?" said Guelvada.

O'Mara yawned. "Ernest," he asked, "have you any blank *cartes d'identités*—properly stamped—with you?"

Guelvada nodded. "I have a dozen of practically everything. Mr. Quayle laid them on. The ones I have are Paris 18ieme Arrondissement cards."

"Good," said O'Mara. "Fill in the card with the name of Taudrille. You'd better make up a Christian name."

"That is not necessary," said Tanga. "His supposed names were, I remember, Jules Francois Taudrille."

"Right," said O'Mara. "Tanga, this concerns you. In an hour or so Mr. Quayle is coming through with some information. He is laying on a contact with the Second Bureau; also the name of the local Resistance or *Maquis* leader in these parts; someone on whom we can rely for local support if we want it. When you've got the Second Bureau contact, make an enquiry. Find out what Taudrille was supposed to be, that is if they know anything about him. Usually, Nazis who were stuck in Concentration Camps for a purpose took the name of a good Resistance or Secret Service Frenchman who had been caught and shot. Taudrille may have done that."

Tanga said: "He did do that. When Epps first talked of him to me, I asked the usual questions and for a description. Epps gave me a photograph of Taudrille—one of the small film pictures that Resistance people carried with their record and identity on the back. The sort of thing they used to stick under cancelled postage stamps on old envelopes and carry when they were moving to a different group. Epps gave me that. I had an enlargement made just before I left Paris for Brieuc. I have it here. Taudrille was, according to the record, one of the first Resistance people; he was supposed to have served with the French Army; the *Contre Espionage Bureau* and the original *Maquis* group."

"Good," O'Mara repeated. "Taudrille was running true to form. The original Taudrille was, I'll bet my last shilling, caught and shot, and our Taudrille took his identity and has been getting away with it ever since. And why not? It's been easier since the war was over than it was during the war."

He turned to Guelvada. "Get the enlarged picture of the film-photo from Tanga," he said. "Put it in an old envelope addressed to Taudrille at some Paris address. Fix a cancelled stamp on the envelope to make it look good. Also fill in Taudrille's name on the *carte d'identité*. Wait until it gets dark to-night; after midnight would be the safest time; there is never anybody about then. Walk round the estuary, and about one hundred yards on this side from the church you'll find the cliff has fallen, making a sort of path down to the rocks. Climb down; turn right and you'll find what's left of Taudrille lying on a flat rock. It's away from the tide, so you'll be able to see if anyone has moved it. Search the body— you'd better take some rubber gloves with you—and put the *carte d'identité* and the photograph in the envelope in an inner pocket.

I don't suppose you'll find anything that matters on the body. He would have been too clever for that, but you never know."

"And then?" asked Guelvada.

"Leave Taudrille where he is," said O'Mara. "But you'd better have a look at his car. It's parked behind the high hedge on the grass verge on the far side of the church. It can stay there. It's in the story. But there might be something, though I doubt it. And get back here before anyone gets a chance to spot you. To-morrow, Tanga can hire the sailing boat from Pontienne. She can hire him and his boat to take her for a sail on the estuary. In the afternoon the tide runs towards the church. Pontienne will come back that way and tack across from there. Tanga will see the body from the boat. She can be looking at the shore with field-glasses. She will tell Pontienne, and when they land, Pontienne will telephone the police at Saint Lys. The police will come to Saint-Brieuc to make an inspection of the body and there will be talk. I want that."

Tanga said: "Is one permitted to ask why?"

O'Mara said: "Taudrille was working with somebody who knew the Saint-Brieuc-Saint Lys district. He must have been. That somebody couldn't have been either Morosc or Nago, because he intended to kill both of them. Which he has done. So it has to be an additional person. And it is probably the person who picked up Nago after he got away and took him to Saint Lys by car."

Tanga said: "I do not wish to be difficult, but if Nago's car was unharmed, why did he not drive it himself to Saint Lys?"

O'Mara said: "Because Taudrille told him not to. Taudrille wanted that car in addition to his own. Can't you guess why?"

She shook her head.

"Taudrille intended to finish me off after he had found where my friends were—after he has discovered where this Villa was. Unfortunately for him, I thought of it first and finished *him*. If he had got rid of me he still had to dispose of the body of Morosc, which is lying in an empty bombed *chateau* on the Saint-Brieuc-Saint Lys road. He would have waited until it was dark and then he would have collected the body of Morosc in the car, driven back to the church, put my corpse in the passenger seat; started the car and let it run over the cliff."

"Exactly," said Guelvada.

"Remember," said O'Mara, "that from first to last—if he plays this thing the right way—our Taudrille is on a good wicket. Remember that he is supposed to be a good Frenchman—a member of the Resistance. Epps believes that. Tanga believed it. There was no reason why she shouldn't. He has the identity and record of a decent Frenchman, and he is on a sure thing if he can get rid of the bodies of Morosc, Nago and the supposed Philippe Garenne in the right way. This is the way he would think."

He held out his hand for another cigarette; waited until it was lit; then: "Nago and Morosc will eventually be known to be Nazi agents. It will be known that they arrived at the *Garage Volanon* during the afternoon, and that no one was there but the stupid Philippe Garenne, who was, as usual, half drunk. Nago and Morosc knew that Garenne was none other than O'Mara, an ex-agent of the British Secret Service, from whom they hoped to extract information. They took Garenne—or O'Mara—away with them; they took him to the deserted *chateau* on the Saint-Brieuc-Saint Lys road for the purpose of putting the screw on him and making him talk. They made him talk. Then they killed him."

Guelvada said: "All this is reasonable. That is normal Nazi routine."

"Precisely," O'Mara continued. "Afterwards there is trouble between Nago and Morosc. That also is reasonable. Nago was a drug addict; he was in bad health; both he and Morosc were working in a country that was no longer at war and where the *Maquis* were on the look-out all the time for old and new enemies. Nago was fed up with Morosc. Also there would be payment for the information extracted from O'Mara and there would be more for him if he had not to share it with Morosc. That is how Taudrille would reason."

"That is understood," said Guelvada.

"So Nago is now supposed to have shot Morosc. He sees that the estuary road and the cliff path are deserted—as they invariably are. He loads the bodies of Morosc and O'Mara on to the car, drives along the cliff path, jumps off the car and allows it to go over the cliff. So much for Morosc and O'Mara."

He inhaled from his cigarette. "Now Nago walks across country to Saint Lys, When he gets there he is tired and depressed. He needs a dose of his own particular drug and he hasn't got it. He knows that something will happen as a result of the bodies being found. He comes to the conclusion that he has had enough of the whole business, so he goes to the little wood behind the *depot* at Saint Lys and shoots himself with his little pistol, after writing a suicide note first of all saving that he is afraid of the *Maquis*.

"That," said O'Mara, "was how Taudrille had worked it out. It would have been a good story. If he had arrived here at the Villa and told that story to Tanga—if he had told her that he had arrived late; that Nago, Morosc and O'Mara had already left the *Garage Volanon*; that when he got to the *chateau* he merely found evidences of trouble in the shape of bloodstains; and afterwards, looking about the neighbourhood, he found the smashed car with the bodies of Morosc and O'Mara on the rocks—she would have believed him. She would have believed that Nago was responsible."

Tanga said: "That is true. I had no reason to suspect Taudrille."

"Of course not," said O'Mara. "Then, when the suicide of Nago is discovered, *and* his note, Taudrilles' story is confirmed, and he would have been on a damned good wicket. He would be, possibly, the only person alive who knew who and where Quayle was, and he would be inside the organisation; next to Tanga; waiting for his chance to strike again. Well . . .?"

Guelvada said: "Of course you are right. It all adds up. That is what Taudrille would have planned. Directly he had killed you he would have arranged it like that. It would have been an excellent story."

"There is only one thing," said Tanga. "You say, O'Mara, that Taudrille would have considered himself to be the only person knowing the information extracted from you. That would be so unless Nago gave that information to some person who was waiting to pick him up and to take him to Saint Lys."

O'Mara nodded. He smiled at Tanga. He said: "The lady has brains. That is why we are going to play it this way. I think there is someone else. I think that Taudrille knew there was someone else. In fact I should not be surprised if he had not himself arranged for Nago to be picked up."

Guelvada said: "I see everything. It is necessary that we find that person. And quickly."

"To-morrow," said O'Mara, "after Ernest here has had a look at the departed Taudrille, you, Tanga, had better telephone through to Pontienne. Tell him that if the weather is fine—and it ought to be—you want to go sailing in his boat round the estuary. Tell him that you want to start about two o'clock in the afternoon. Tell him that he and his boat were recommended to you by Philippe Garenne at the *Garage Volanon*. Take some field-glasses with you and, when you are tacking back, across the estuary, put up your glasses, find the place where the cliff face has fallen in; look to the left and discover Taudrille's body. Then tell Pontienne and get him to sail in so that you get a closer look."

Guelvada said: "Madame la Comtesse, it seems that we are to have an amusing time."

She smiled at him. She said: "Yes . . . amusing, possibly exciting."

They looked at O'Mara. He was fast asleep.

She said: "He can be very annoying. I wished to say good night."

Guelvada was enjoying himself.

As the clock in the little church tower struck one, he drove the Typhoon into the shadow of the yew trees at the end farthest from the road. He stood, silently regarding the long and powerful car, smoking a cigarette, wondering whether he should inspect Taudrille's body or Taudrille's car.

He decided that the car could wait. He threw the cigarette away; walked across the small churchyard on to the cliff path. He moved quickly and silently, humming softly to himself.

He came to the cliff path, began to descend. The moon was up and only a slight breeze that swished gently through the yew trees broke the stillness of a lovely night.

Guelvada began to think about Taudrille. He wondered who Taudrille was; what his real name had been; what sort of a man he was. Probably the usual sort of person doing the usual sort of thing that Himmler-trained people did; yet, thought Guelvada, even these near robots of the Nazi system must have some sort of individuality; some sort of life of their own. Guelvada, whose mind liked to move off at occasional tangents, amused himself by a consideration of what might have been the inside and private story of Taudrille. Of his background, his home, his women—if there had been women.

By now he was at the bottom of the path. The waters of the estuary lapped the sandy shore fifty yards away. To his right stretched the uneven pathway of rocks, flat, creviced; dangerous for walking. Guelvada, who walked as securely as a cat, turned to the right and began to make his way along the base of the cliff, keeping to the shadow.

He came upon the body suddenly. It lay on a flat rock, half obscured by a larger rock. Guelvada drew closer to the cliff, lit a cigarette, smoked silently, looking at the broken body that lay before him.

So that was Taudrille. And it might have been O'Mara. That was what Taudrille had planned to do to O'Mara. But it hadn't come off because O'Mara was lucky and for half a dozen other reasons.

Guelvada began to think of the stories he had heard of O'Mara. Most of them were true. Being killed was a thing that did not happen to O'Mara. *Nearly* being killed; being hi-jacked, slugged, an occasional spot of torture; all the concomitants of death were things that had happened, and did happen, to O'Mara. Only the ultimate thing had not happened. Probably, Guelvada thought, because O'Mara was too clever, and when his natural cleverness was of no avail he had that supreme companion—luck.

Guelvada began to think of the middle days of the war; when he had been working in Lisbon with, first of all, Kane, and then with Michael Kells—one of Quayle's most subtle operatives. Guelvada had heard lots of stories of O'Mara in those days. He was practically a legend amongst the strange tribe of Britons who worked secretly against the Nazi menace that stalked, almost openly at one time, in that part of the world. He remembered how O'Mara had been given a Mickey Finn, slugged, locked in a small watertight cellar with the water turned on. Ninety-nine men out of a hundred would have "had it," Guelvada reflected, but not O'Mara.

The hundred-to-one chance came off; the house next door caught fire; the fire brigade, concerned with hydrants, searched for the deflected current of water and O'Mara was discovered, unconscious, with his nose barely above the surface.

That was luck. That was the sort of luck to have with you. O'Mara had it.

And he had other things too. A sublime nonchalance, coupled with an unbreakable nerve, a brain that was cunning to the point of brilliancy and an instinct that worked when everything else failed. Someone or other had once said of O'Mara, that he had "the courage of a lion, the cunning of a snake and the instinct of a woman."

Guelvada grinned. He thought that was a nice combination. He hoped it would work.

He looked at the illuminated dial of his wrist-watch. It was twenty minutes past one and time to go to work.

He took off his jacket, slipped on the rubber surgeon's gloves; began his unpleasant task. Five minutes' careful work showed him O'Mara's guess had been right. There was nothing of importance on the body. A cigarette lighter, a cigarette case and fountain pen—both of which had been smashed by the fall; a roll of bloodstained hundred and five-hundred franc notes.

Guelvada inserted his fingers into the top waistcoat pocket under the soiled jacket—the pocket into which O'Mara had inserted Taudrille's copy of the suicide note. It was empty. The note was gone.

Guelvada straightened up; rolled off the gloves; turned them inside out and put them in the pocket of his jacket. He put on the jacket; stood, looking down at the body.

This, he thought, was one of those things. Definitely one of those things. The little thing that happened and upset all preconceived notions and calculations. Someone had been sufficiently interested in the late Taudrille to search the body—an extremely unpleasant process—and to remove the note. And what would be the idea behind that?

Only one idea was possible. Whoever had done the searching had decided that it was not indicated that Taudrille should appear to be a suicide.

An extremely inconvenient person, thought Guelvada. O'Mara's idea had been obvious. The suicide note discovered on Taudrille's body would cover a multitude of sins. Even when the body was inspected by the Saint Lys police at the instigation of Pontienne, who was to discover it later, with Tanga, according to O'Mara's plan, the discovery of the note would enable the police to "write off" the body as a suicide without taking further trouble. If they *wanted* to take trouble and get into touch with Paris for a thorough check on the supposed Taudrille they would have forwarded to Headquarters the record and photograph which Guelvada had already inserted in the used envelope, and which he had intended to leave on the body. Headquarters would have found, through the Second Bureau, that Taudrille was a fake, impersonating the *real* Taudrille, who had been a French *agent* and who was now dead.

And after that the police would have allowed the matter to drop. They would have taken the suicide note at its face value. They would have considered that the fake Taudrille had been "eliminated" by the *Maquis,* or one of the Resistance groups who had known the truth, and who had "eliminated" quite a lot of people since the war had ended.

The matter of the dead supposed Taudrille would have been allowed to drop—except that there would have been some sort of superficial enquiry which would have achieved the purpose that O'Mara had in mind—that of drawing public attention to the discovery of the corpse—and that would have been that.

But now? Guelvada stood, the envelope in his hand; the envelope that contained the enlarged film photograph of Taudrille and his supposed record with the French Army, the *Contre-Espionage* Section and the *Maquis*. The discovery of this on the body *without* the suicide note might have an entirely different effect; might produce an entirely different result from what O'Mara intended.

Guelvada thought for a moment; then decided. He would leave the envelope. When O'Mara heard the news, if he decided against it, it would have to be removed somehow before the police got to the body.

Guelvada bent over the body; slipped the envelope into the inside breast pocket of the jacket. He made his way over the rocks, back to the cliff path. As he climbed the path he whistled softly to himself. It was an old Belgian tune, and the words which went with it, roughly translated, said that whatever was going to happen would happen, and so whatever you did or thought, wouldn't really make much difference.

The small ivory clock on the mantelpiece showed Quayle that it was twenty-five minutes past one. He reached out his hand to the bed-table for a cigarette; lit it; lay on his back, looking at the ceiling, thinking.

He was dressed in a pair of blue silk pyjamas and a thin silk dressing-gown. His bulk caused the bed to sag in the middle. He lay quite still, his eyes fixed on the ceiling, trying to make a mental picture of Rozanski.

It was always easier if you knew what the man looked like. If you knew what the man looked like—the cut of his features, the shape of his jaw, his eyes, his lips, his general expression—you knew something about him; you could guess things. You could draw pictures in your mind of the type of woman who would attract him and who would be attracted by him; you could consider his reactions to certain circumstances; his temperament. With luck you might even be able—Quayle smiled a little at the thought—to work out something about his blood pressure; his ability to hold liquor and his general mental reactions.

But he knew nothing of Rozanski's appearance. And very little of Rozanski. He knew Rozanski only by what he had done. And, thought Quayle, he was doing very well in the circumstances.

Rozanski, Quayle considered, must have been possessed of a certain cool desperation. There was nothing in anything for him. There was certainly no escape. With the war over, and the tooth-comb being drawn again and again throughout the world, picking up each time, here and there, yet another Nazi who thought he might have escaped the drag-net, Rozanski must have known that there was no future for him. But he was not concerned with the future. He was concerned with the present. He intended to make the greatest use of the present.

And he had not done so badly. He had managed to "liquidate"—that word that the Germans liked so much—no less than four of Quayle's more important agents working in the Gouarec area. But he had *not* known that the last to die—Mullaly, an Anglo-Irishman with a developed sense of humour that was not to be thwarted by the cold and nearby hand of death—had scrawled, in his last moments, on an envelope, a cynical equation: *"Marion, Ewart, Hugo, Patrick, plus Rozanski, equals This."*

Quayle had looked at the soiled envelope and understood. The Christian names stood for Marion Doradel, Ewart Francis, Hugo Mayne and Patrick Mullaly. Plus Rozanski they had equalled This—which was Death.

Quayle had started to dig on the name Rozanski. He had found out a little. He allowed his mind to wander along the pathway that had been the life of Rozanski. First of all the young German cavalry officer, full of life, of ardour, of *esprit de corps,* of—possibly—chivalry. Then the accident which had necessitated his transfer from his own regiment—a transfer which had probably embittered him.

Then his life as an Intelligence Officer in the 1914-18 War—the last Gentleman's War—when Intelligence was just that, and mainly concerned with indexes and records; then the Peace and the coming of the Nazi *régime.*

Quayle wondered how Rozanski had liked that *régime.* Probably he did not like it—*at first.* Most of the old type German Regular Officers had disliked it—*at first.* Afterwards, they had learned that it was a good thing to like it; that life, under the *régime,* could still offer rewards. Almost in spite of themselves, they had begun to believe in it. Rozanski certainly had. Then, finally, like the rest of them, he had been carried forward on the wave of enthusiasm for the domination of the world by German arms; had, at first, almost involuntarily, then willingly, subscribed to the peculiar ethics of the S.S. Intelligence Schools; then to the even more peculiar and cynical teachings of the Himmler Training Academies for External and Internal Agents. Eventually he had become Rozanski—a name that stood for a method, a system, that eventually spelled death for anyone foolish enough to oppose it.

Rozanski, thought Quayle, would go down fighting. There was no future for him. There remained for him only revenge on the enemies of the system of which he was a part. Those enemies who had, by some strange quibble of fate, managed to beat the system. Merely by luck of course. . . .

Quayle heaved himself up from the bed, stubbed out the half-smoked cigarette, sat on the edge of the bed, looking at the unlit electric fire.

He had baited the hook for Rozanski. He had baited the hook with such succulent bait that Rozanski—even in spite of himself—must strike. Because the bait was so tempting.

And what bait! First of all O'Mara—the best agent ever employed in his country's service. First of all O'Mara on a plate; then, when the strike had missed, O'Mara, Guelvada and Tanga de Sarieux. Three splendidly trained, experienced, dyed-in-the wool espionage and counter-espionage agents, who, during the war years, had struck again and again at the very heart of Germany and had each time drawn blood. Rozanski could not ignore such bait.

Quayle thought of the three. He shrugged his shoulders. He hoped that once again they would be as successful. You could not make omelettes without breaking eggs. And if it was necessary that they be broken, those three eggs were tough specimens that did not break easily.

It was characteristic of Quayle that he did not include himself in the omelette, although by this time Rozanski would know of his existence; would certainly take all possible steps to end it.

The buzzer on the inter-communicating telephone sounded. Quayle went over to the desk; picked up the receiver.

Myra said: "Mr. Quayle, I've taken the note from the Second Bureau. Your idea about the original Taudrille was right. I've the record here and the name of the local *Maquis* group leader in the Gouarec area. Also one of the 'M' departments wants you, please. They called through the contact number."

Quayle said: "All right. I'll come along now."

He went out of the bedroom, along a passage, through a sitting-room at the end; through another passage into the flat kitchen. He opened a cupboard door; pushed at the back of the cupboard; went through into the room on the other side.

The room was large and furnished with two desks and a dozen large steel filing cabinets. The walls were covered with large-scale maps of the Breton coast and shore areas. There were half a dozen telephones grouped on the mantelpiece. Myra sat at her desk, the switchboard at her right hand.

Quayle said: "You look tired."

"I am tired," she said. "That damned moving job wasn't so hot. But Eleanor comes on in half an hour."

Quayle nodded. He asked: "Who wanted me from 'M?'"

"Colonel Mason," she answered. "He's been through twice. The first time I thought you were asleep. He said it wasn't frightfully important."

Quayle nodded. He said: "You'd better get him."

She dialled a number. After a minute, she pushed the plug in the switchboard. She said: "Number three."

Quayle took up one of the receivers on the mantelpiece. He said: "Hello . . . Mason?" He listened. Eventually he said: "No . . . he won't talk. They never do. And we aren't allowed to go to work on them. I suppose they'll hang him in due course." He hung up. He stood leaning against the mantelpiece, his hands in his dressing-gown pockets.

After a little while he said: "We got out of Pall Mall just at the right moment."

Myra raised an eyebrow. She asked: "Did something happen?"

He nodded. "The fellow who took over our offices was a Pole," he said. "The representative in England of some firm or other. He was late at the offices to-night. Moving in, I suppose; putting his things straight."

"Yes?" she said. She looked anxiously at Quayle.

"He came out of the offices somewhere about midnight," said Quayle, "and turned towards St. James's Street. He was shot within twenty yards of the office entrance. Mason tells me that he was rather like me in appearance."

"Is he dead?" she asked.

Quayle nodded. "The police have picked up a man already," he said. "He says he's a Yugoslav or something like that. He has no papers and can't explain his presence in England. He's not even trying to. He won't talk. They found a pistol on him. If the bullets match up he'll hang."

She said: "They meant to get you. You'll have to be careful."

Quayle said: "Why?"

She did not answer.

He said: "Get through to the Countess and give her that stuff from Second Bureau and the name and address of the *Maquis* bloke at Gouarec. Whenever you talk to them from now on, use the date number check. You give them a number which is the date of the month plus the number of the day of the week. The Countess gives you back the date plus the number of the day plus three; Guelvada plus two; O'Mara plus one."

"What about the maid Yvette?" asked Myra.

"Don't worry about her. She won't be using the telephone from now on," said Quayle. "They'll know in a minute that they're on the top line. Good night."

He went away.

She began to dial for the Paris number. The door on the far side of the room opened. Eleanor Frayne, her relief, came in. She was a tall, fair girl who looked vaguely stupid. She told her friends that she was studying interior decorating and took a great interest in the ballet. She cultivated the pose of stupidity. She was one of Quayle's four secretaries who worked the clock round with him.

Myra said: "One of the 'M' Departments has been through. A Pole, who took over our offices and who looks rather like Quayle, was shot coming out of the place to-night."

Eleanor produced a mirror from her handbag and began to tidy her hair.

She said: "Papa Quayle will have to be careful, won't he?"

"I told him so," said Myra. "He said 'Why?'"

"Quite," said Eleanor.

Myra got up from the switchboard. She went to a locker, got out her coat. She began to put it on. She said: "What the hell do you mean by 'quite?'"

"What I said," said Eleanor. "And I said 'quite.'" She lisped a little—quite attractively. "If you do the sort of job that Quayle does, how the devil *can* you be careful?"

Myra put on her hat. She said: "Good night."

"Good night, darling," said Eleanor. "And go straight home, sweet."

Myra said cynically: "I suppose you think that somebody might shoot *me!*"

"No, dear," said Eleanor. "I was thinking of wandering wolves of the male sex. You look good enough to eat."

Myra said: "Nuts!" Not unpleasantly. She went on: "Paris will be on in a minute. There's some information to be passed on. There's a cut-out line to a number in Saint-Brieuc. It's all on the pad. The *Villa Cote d'Azur.* O'Mara, Guelvada, de Sarieux. The check number is the date, plus the number of the day of the week, plus one for O'Mara, two for Guelvada and three for the Countess. Got that?"

Eleanor said: "I'm ahead of you."

Myra closed the door gently behind her. Eleanor changed the plug in the switchboard—a habit she had developed—she did not quite know why; opened the desk drawer. She took out a thriller and began to read.

She liked thrillers.

The church clock struck two as Guelvada reached the cliff path. His mind was still busy with possibilities; searching for some motive as to why anybody should have been sufficiently interested in Taudrille to remove the suicide note. At what time had the note been removed? Guelvada walked along the cliff path, across the churchyard; skirted the yew-tree grove; walked down the road; found the grass verge hidden by the high bushes where Taudrille's car still stood.

He went to the other side of the bushes; looked up and down the road. There was no one in sight. Guelvada returned to the car; got into it; produced a pencil torch from his pocket; began to examine the floor of the car.

A low, tremulous voice said: "You filthy swine. So I've found you."

Guelvada sighed. It was most inconvenient, he thought, at this time that anything untoward should happen. He straightened up; got out of the car; stood on the grass verge. Just in front of him, standing in the shadow caused by the bushes, was a young woman—a very charming young woman, Guelvada thought, despite the fact that she was extremely angry; despite the fact that at the moment the automatic pistol which she held in her hand was pointing directly at his navel.

He said softly: "Mademoiselle, it may easily be that I am a swine, although I doubt that, but I am definitely not filthy. I bath considerably."

She said: "Filthy murdering swine. I would like to kill you. It would give me a great deal of pleasure to kill you, but I am not going to do that. I am going to hand you over to the police. I shall love to think that you will be hanged or guillotined—preferably hanged."

Guelvada said: "I am sorry about that." He shrugged his shoulders. "Of the two methods I should most certainly prefer to be guillotined." He spoke slowly, coolly, quite dispassionately, but his eyes were searching. The girl, he thought, was about twenty-eight years of age. He raised the narrow beam of the torch so that some illumination fell upon her. She was quite pretty. Her face was oval and white, and the angry eyes, which looked at him almost viciously, were brown. In repose, Guelvada thought, her features would be admirable. As it was, at the moment, they were distorted by an intense rage. A very virile and vital person, he thought.

He said: "Mademoiselle, I would like you to tell me whom I have murdered. You know, it is very easy to make mistakes, especially when one is bad tempered."

She said: "I know about you. I can guess about you. You're one of those filthy Nazis—one of those people who have not yet been caught—who are still wandering about our country trying even now, in spite of everything, to make more mischief. Jules has told me about what sort of people you are."

Guelvada said: "I see. So Jules told you—Jules Francois Taudrille. Mademoiselle, am I permitted to ask what he was to you?"

She almost hissed: "You will find out. He was the man I love— the man I intend to avenge. Before he came here to Saint Brieuc, he told me of the sort of things that might happen to him. He told me of the dangers of the work he was doing. He warned me of what he might expect from people like you."

Guelvada saw that there were tears in her eyes. For some reason which he could not quite explain to himself he conceived the idea that this young woman was deriving a certain amount of pleasure from the scene—almost as if it were part of a play. An idea leapt into his agile mind—the idea that this girl was a professional actress; that, in spite of the fact that she had loved Taudrille; that she really proposed to do something about his death; in spite of all that, she was being carried away by what was after all a very good leading part.

Guelvada said: "I would be very grateful if you would allow me to smoke a cigarette, and I would also be grateful if you would not point that automatic pistol at my stomach. I am unarmed and entirely at your mercy." He smiled benignly at her; produced a loose cigarette from his pocket; lit it.

He said: "Mademoiselle, perhaps you will be good enough to tell me why you think I killed your lover."

"Why should I answer the questions of the son of a pig?" she asked. "Why should I do that when all the time I am impatient to shoot you in the stomach and then, whilst you are still alive and wriggling, to smash in your face with the butt of this pistol? Do you think that you will gain time by asking questions?"

Guelvada said almost archly: "Mademoiselle, you will agree with me that any man is justified in trying to gain a little time before being shot in the stomach and having his face smashed in. But you will not do anything at all like that. You will not do it because such an act would be entirely foreign to your nature. Instead, you will tell me, if you please, why you are under the mistaken impression that I have killed Taudrille."

She said: "Why should I argue with you—you self-satisfied dog? It is quite obvious to me why you killed Jules. He was supposed to come back to Saint Lys and see me. He promised me he would come back after he had finished his work in Saint Brieuc. I knew it was dangerous. When he did not come back I worried. I knew that his mission had brought him somewhere near this church. So to-night I came here on my bicycle. I came here because I could no longer wait, worrying desperately about him. And I found the motor car. I waited here for a long time hoping that he would come back. But the engine was cold. I knew the car had been standing here for a long while."

Guelvada raised his eyebrows. He said: "You would have made an excellent detective."

She said: "Don't talk. Don't interrupt me, because I could very easily kill you now."

"No doubt," said Guelvada, "but I assure you that it wouldn't do me any good, and it certainly wouldn't do *you* any good. So you came here and found the car. And then?"

"Then I walked along the cliff top," she said. I walked along the path and found the place where the cliff had fallen in. I went down to the rocks . . ."

Guelvada could see the tears running down her face.

"And I found him . . . my poor Jules. . . ."

Guelvada said sorrowfully: "Mademoiselle, I assure you that I sympathise very deeply with you. Permit me to tell you that. If you will listen to me I shall be able to prove to you in a moment that I was in no way responsible for the death of Monsieur Taudrille. I *think* I shall be able to prove that."

He looked at her. His face radiated such benignity; such a charming smile played around his mouth, that in spite of herself a shadow of doubt crossed her face.

Guelvada said: "Permit me to ask *you* one or two questions, Mademoiselle. I take it that when you went down to the rocks and discovered the remains of your unfortunate lover, you were brave enough to search the body?"

She said: "Yes, I did. He had promised, if by any chance he could not get back to Saint Lys to keep his appointment with me late last night—"

Guelvada interrupted quickly. "After the theatrical performance was over?" he hazarded.

"So," she said softly in her attractive low voice. "So . . . you give yourself away. You have been watching us. Jules said that you were watching; said that he was surrounded all the time by hateful eyes that never left him. If this is not true, how did you know that I am an actress? Answer me that."

Guelvada said: "Mademoiselle, you radiate the theatre. I think you are quite wonderful. On the stage you would be marvellous. You could not prevent something of the theatre showing itself in your face, in your every gesture. I guessed it . . . but forgive the interruption. So M'sieu Taudrille promised you if he could not get back and keep an appointment with you after the performance at Saint Lys . . . then what?"

She said: "He promised he would send me a note. I thought he might have written the note. I thought he might have indicated something which would enable me to track down his murderers." She said: "I know that someone threw him over that cliff. He was very clever, very brave. He would never have fallen over accidentally. He had a superb instinct. I know he was murdered."

Guelvada said: "I have no doubt, Mademoiselle, that you are absolutely right. And so you searched the body because you hoped to find the note which he had written to you but which he had not been able to despatch, and you were unable to find it?"

She nodded. Now she was holding the pistol in her hand, which hung straight down by her side. Guelvada thought that, carried away as she was by her emotion, it would be fairly easy for him to take it from her. He thought the process was unnecessary.

"And then?" asked Guelvada.

She said: "Then I found something which made me certain that he had been killed. In the top pocket of his waistcoat I found a note which said that he was afraid of the *Maquis*; a suggestion that he was seeking relief from his fears by suicide."

Guelvada said: "Of course an entirely ridiculous idea, Mademoiselle. But tell me, because I may be able to be of use to you, why the idea was so ridiculous? Was it quite impossible that M'sieu Taudrille should be afraid of the *Maquis*?"

She said in a low sibilant voice: "You fool . . . why should *he* be afraid of the *Maquis*—he who was an incomparable *agent* in the service of France—who had himself been one of the original organisers of the *Maquis* groups in this country—who had fought tooth and nail against the Germans. My brave . . . brave Jules. . . . Why should *he* have been afraid of the *Maquis*?"

Guelvada said: "Of course. I see it all now. You are entirely correct. There is no doubt that he has been deliberately murdered by someone who is working for the Nazis."

She said: "That is so, M'sieu. And why should that person not be you?"

Guelvada sat down on the running-board of Taudrille's car. He drew on his cigarette. He was perfectly at ease.

He said: "I can assure you, Mademoiselle, that I shall prove to you in a minute that it was not I. I shall do that very easily . . . now we have elucidated the fact that you found this suicide note, and you removed it. You removed it because you knew that it had been put into his pocket merely as a blind. It had been put there to delude the police when the body was eventually found. It was hoped that this note would make them believe that Taudrille was one of those traitors who have met a well-deserved fate at the hands of some of the brave people who did so much for France and who have suffered so much during the last few years. That is what you thought, isn't it?"

She said: "Of course."

Guelvada looked up at her; his blue eyes were wide; his face presented the picture of a man who in no circumstances could tell a lie.

He said: "Mademoiselle, I ask you to listen carefully to me. I know that everything you say is true. I know that, because I was Jules Taudrille's assistant—his colleague. I too was waiting for him to return to Saint Lys, where he was to see me. I too knew the dangers which he would encounter here in Saint Brieuc. Like you, I came here to-night, knowing that he had an appointment near this church; to try and find a clue as to what had happened."

She said: "Is this true? Can I believe this?"

Guelvada said: "I'm going to prove it to you in a moment, Mademoiselle. You must realise that, no matter how deep you were in the confidence of my dear friend Jules, there were still some things which he could not tell you—secrets which belong only to him and France—secrets of which only I—his friend, companion and colleague—had merely an inkling. Like you, I am desirous only of finding his murderer, whom I will kill with my hands."

Guelvada rose dramatically to his feet. He said: "Mademoiselle, I will now prove to you that what I say is correct; that I have told you the truth. When, like you, I found the path down to the rocks to-night; when I realised that that place down there—protected from sight from above and on each side—was an ideal place for the secret meeting which I knew Jules was attending with some people of whom I knew little, I went down there. I found his body. Like you, I searched it, but"—Guelvada drew himself up to his full height—"I did not remove anything from the body, Mademoiselle. I left something on it. I left something on it which, when I show it to you, will prove to you that I was the friend of your lover. I left something on it for the police to find; something which will make them more than keen to assist me in the search for his murderer."

Guelvada stopped talking. He felt that his last speech had been very good indeed.

She asked: "What did you leave? Tell me."

Guelvada said: "Mademoiselle, you may not know, but every agent in the French Service was in the habit of carrying with him a tiny micro-photograph of himself. Superimposed on a backing on the photographic film was his record, so that wherever he went he would be able to identify himself to friends. I had seen that micro-photograph of my friend Taudrille. I myself had made an enlargement of it—an enlargement which was a duplicate of one kept at our headquarters in Paris. I left that photograph, Mademoiselle, on the body. If you will come down with me you will find it there."

She looked at him. Her mouth drooped a little. Guelvada realised that she had swallowed the story, hook, line and sinker.

She said: "M'sieu, I am beginning to believe you. I would like to see this photograph."

Guelvada said: "Come with me."

He led the way out of the shadows, across the churchyard to the cliff path. When they had gone a little way he put out his hand and took the automatic pistol from her. She surrendered it willingly. He could see the tears running down her face. He put the pistol in the inside pocket of his jacket. He walked silently beside her. The breeze from the sea came towards them. Guelvada opened his mouth and inhaled it. He was thinking that Taudrille must have been pretty good.

Definitely, thought Guelvada, Taudrille had been very good indeed.

O'Mara awakened. He lay, blinking, trying to accustom his eyes to the sunlight that flooded through the long windows. He stretched lazily.

Life, mused O'Mara, could present a peculiar conglomeration of circumstances at the slightest provocation. And sometimes without even the provocation. Not so very long ago he had been giving an imitation of what the Americans call a playboy in Copacabana, Rio de Janeiro. He had told himself that so far as Quayle was concerned he could—at any rate until someone else decided to start a war—say good-bye to trouble. That is what he had *thought*.

And then Quayle had decided to send a cable and everything went haywire. Everything that mattered. Or did it? O'Mara wondered whether it mattered very greatly. Whether Rio mattered, or the beautiful Eulalia or anything else. Did he really mind? He thought that he was not quite certain as to the answer to that one. In any event, it had been good-bye to all that. And now he was lying in some other woman's bed—he wondered what Eulalia would have to say to that—with three burned fingers and a problem to which he was to find some sort of solution.

He allowed his mind to wander. He thought it would be damned funny if Eulalia—for reasons best known to herself—

decided to come to Saint Brieuc for a holiday and discovered him; discovered that he was living in a charming villa set in its own delightful grounds, with a beautiful woman in the vicinity. What would Eulalia think?

O'Mara grinned. He thought he knew the answer to *that* one. He thought that there might be a lot of trouble. He wondered just what Eulalia would *do* about it. . . decided that he did not know, and, as the situation had not arisen and was not likely to arise, did not care.

He came back to the present. He considered circumstances.

His left hand had been redressed. It felt comfortable and the bandages were fresh. Tanga de Sarieux, he thought, had been in during the night and fixed it whilst he was sleeping. He got out of bed and tried his foot. He found he could walk without much discomfort.

He got back into bed.

The time had come, thought O'Mara, when something definite had to be done. Something definite that would start a train of events that would eventually bring about a situation. The sort of situation in which something very practical could be done. He thought immediately of Ernest Guelvada. He wondered why it was that one associated practicality with Ernest. He shrugged his shoulders. Possibly the answer was that Guelvada was an extraordinarily *neat* worker with any sort of lethal weapon.

Somehow, somewhere, Rozanski had to be dug up and disposed of, O'Mara thought. Somewhere Rozanski was sitting planning death and disaster—a macabre celebration of his own approaching end. O'Mara had agreed with Quayle that Rozanski would reason that he had not long for this earth, but that when he left it he would depart in a blaze of death and glory, and take with him as many of his old-time enemies as he could. Plus any other people who got in the way.

There was a knock on the door. O'Mara said: "Come in."

Tanga came into the room. She put the breakfast tray she carried on to the bedside table. Then she drew up a chair, sat down and began to pour O'Mara's coffee.

She said: "Good morning, O'Mara. Did you sleep well?"

He nodded. He wondered why she called him O'Mara. He thought it funny that quite a number of women had, in his adult lifetime, for some occult reason known only to themselves, dispensed with his Christian name; contented themselves with calling him O'Mara. He thought about this and found no answer.

He took the cup from her. He noticed her long slim fingers; the beautifully designed finger-rings. He said: "You did a good job on my hand last night. I must have been sleeping heavily. It feels a lot better."

"You were in a trance," she said. This morning, he thought, her French accent was more pronounced, and quite charming. "But then you were tired—very tired. I was quite glad, because I did not want to disturb you." She smiled suddenly. "Also," she continued, "I thought it would be an excellent time to regard you closely and come to conclusions about your personality and character."

O'Mara finished the coffee; handed her the cup. She refilled it.

He asked: "What were your conclusions?"

She looked at him mischievously. "Personality—one *thinks*—attractive. It *could* be. Character bad—but definitely bad. Not to be trusted by unprotected women."

"Quite," said O'Mara. "Have you the information I wanted?"

"Of course," she said. "Can it be that the more than merely observant O'Mara has not noticed that in addition to being homely and comfortable, I am an extremely hard-working woman, and luckily can exist almost without sleep."

O'Mara grinned. "You have some very good attributes," he said. "I have no doubt about that." He looked at her, took in a picture of the leaf-green linen frock, the slender, gossamer clad legs and ankles, the leaf-green sandals, the loosely-dressed black hair. He caught a picture of the oval face, the tranquil eyes; the raspberry lips that showed small, white teeth.

He continued: "But those attributes don't matter a lot. Why should they? They are almost redundant in a woman as beautiful as you are."

He reached for a cigarette. "What about the Second Bureau contact, and the local *Maquis* leader?"

She looked at him. O'Mara thought he detected a certain quiet insolence in the look; then she dropped her eyes demurely. When she raised them her expression was purely businesslike.

He thought: Quayle certainly does find them. Heaven only knows *how* and *where,* but he does.

She said: "Your Second Bureau contact is Monsieur Guy Varin. The original—the *real*—Taudrille worked in his section. I anticipated that you would want to know something of the record and achievements of the original Taudrille. I have a note of those. Yvette is at this moment typing it out for you. The local *Maquis* leader—who has a distinguished record in the war and has been twice decorated by De Gaulle—is one Jean Marie Larue, who lives at No. 13 Rue des Pêcheurs, at Gouarec. Larue is a photographer by profession and personally killed six Germans during the occupation; besides other distinguished work. He is, it seems, a small and dark Breton who is intelligent and is thoroughly to be trusted. Monsieur Varin is sending a photograph and a replica of the identity card which the *Maquis* use in this part of the country. It will be here to-day."

O'Mara said: "Have you talked to London?"

She nodded her head. "I have talked to Eleanor Frayne," she said. "It seems that someone—described loosely as a Yugoslav—endeavoured to shoot Monsieur Quayle. So the Headquarters are moved. We shall know the address when necessary. The telephone number remains the same, and there is a private line connection between us via Paris. The check numbers are the day of the month plus the day of the week, plus one for you, two for Monsieur Guelvada and three for me."

She flashed a sudden smile at him.

"Monsieur Quayle has the most charming manner of letting one know who is in charge and to whom we look for orders," she said demurely.

O'Mara said casually: "You'd have realised *that* in any event." He lit the cigarette. "Where is Ernest Guelvada?" he asked.

"In the kitchen," she answered. "He arrived back, I believe, at five o'clock this morning. He did not appear at all tired and proceeded to clean the car engine. He went to bed for two hours, and has since been walking about the grounds and discussing rhododendrons with Yvette. At the moment he is setting the blade of a small Swedish sailor's knife on an oilstone. Do you know why he does that?"

O'Mara said: "He carries the knife in his hat. There is a small clip inside it to take the knife. The blade, which disappears into the handle of the knife and which shoots out when the spring is released, is three and a half inches long. Ernest keeps it razor-sharp He can throw the knife better than anyone I've ever known. At ten yards he can pierce the centre of a playing-card. He is very fond of the knife. He says that it is very neat and quick and saves a great deal of trouble."

She said: "Yes? But why does he feel like that?"

O'Mara shrugged his shoulders. "They did something to his girl friend and she died. He didn't like that."

"I understand," she said. "That is probably the reason why he looks so pleasant all the time. He has become tired of hating. He has probably been able to sublimate his hatred by the use of the little knife."

O'Mara grinned. "I shouldn't wonder at that," he said.

There was a silence. Then: "You'd better get some sleep to-night," said O'Mara. "I shall move out of here this morning. Thank you for the use of your bed. And I shall want some clothes."

"Monsieur Varin is sending clothes from Paris," she said. "I arranged that. Two suits and shirts and linen and shoes and toilet things. I gave him the measurements from the clothes you were wearing."

"Good," said O'Mara. He stubbed out his cigarette. "This afternoon it might be a good thing if you drove down to the estuary and had a talk with Volanon. You can tell him that when you saw me there I had arranged to do some small job on the car. You can find out if he is wondering where I am or what has happened to me. You may get some small talk from the village. Volanon is the local rumour merchant. He is always talking. Then later this afternoon, before you rest, you'd better telephone Monsieur Varin and get him to ask the Gouarec police to 'discover' the fake

Taudrille's body. That will save you sailing about the estuary with old Pontienne."

She got up from her chair. She said: "The idea of sailing on the estuary appealed to me. I do not wish particularly to rest this afternoon."

"Maybe not," said O'Mara. "But you will. You may have to work late. You'd better get all the sleep you can."

She smiled at him. Her smiles were sudden. He liked them. She said: "It is good of you to be concerned with my health."

"I'm *not* concerned with your health," said O'Mara. "Not now. I'm concerned with your efficiency whilst this job's on. When it's over I'll begin to worry about your health. And I'd like to see Guelvada."

She said: "Very well." She went to the door. She stopped, turned and looked at him. She said: "You are inclined to be somewhat like a pig at times. But I expect other ladies have also told you that?"

O'Mara nodded his head. He regarded her with equanimity. He said: "Yes . . . they have."

She asked: "Do you like that?"

He shrugged his shoulders. "Why should I mind?" He grinned at her—an impertinent grin. "They always change their opinions," he added.

She raised her eyebrows. "Always?" she queried.

"Always," said O'Mara. He reached for another cigarette.

She stood motionless, looking at him, one hand on the door-knob. She presented a delightful picture.

She asked softly: "Did Eulalia Guimaraes change *her* opinion?"

O'Mara looked at her with narrowed eyes. For a moment his equanimity was almost shaken. He gained time by reaching for the lighter and lighting his cigarette.

He said: "I think that I am safe in saying that the Senhorita Eulalia Guimaraes was never of the opinion that I was inclined to be 'somewhat like a pig at times.'" He stressed the words she had used.

She said: "It must be nice for you to think *that,* O'Mara."

"It *is* nice," said O'Mara. He went on, with a change of voice: "Have a really good talk with Volanon. Find out as much as is possible what the local people think of my disappearance—that is, if they *think* I have disappeared."

"I understand," she said. "I expect your clothes will be here in an hour. Monsieur Varin said that he would send everything by airplane to Quimpere and from there by car. It should arrive at any moment. Will you see Monsieur Guelvada immediately?"

"No," said O'Mara. "I'll wait for the clothes. I'll see him after lunch."

"Very well," she said. "I will tell him that." She opened the door. "You were wrong about Eulalia Guimaraes," she said casually. "Quite wrong." She flashed a demure smile at him.

O'Mara said: "Really . . . it would be very interesting to know *how* I was wrong, Countess." His tone was slightly acid.

She shrugged her shoulders almost imperceptibly. "Eulalia thought you were a little like a pig at times. She told me so. She said that you had many of the qualities of a really nice pig."

There was silence. Then she said in an innocent voice: "Of course she would *know*. She kept some pigs on that charming farm of hers outside Huarjo . . . . I expect you remember. Lunch is at one-thirty and Yvette will show you your new room and the geography of the house. She will bring you a dressing-gown."

She closed the door gently behind her.

O'Mara stubbed out the cigarette. He said to himself: "Well . . . I'll be damned!"

O'Mara stood in front of the pier glass in the bedroom to which Yvette had shown him. He was tying a blue silk tie with difficulty. Guelvada, sitting by the window, looked out on to the drive that ran round both sides of the Villa; smoked and watched O'Mara.

O'Mara said: "Your girl friend of last night must have been quite interesting."

Guelvada said: "Yes . . .! Madame la Comtesse has taste; those clothes might have been made for you. Also they are well cut. She has an eye for detail . . . that one."

O'Mara said: "Even the shaving soap was good. How does she know? Is she married to someone . . . has she been married? Do you know anything about her?"

Guelvada smiled. "I consulted Quayle's information bureau—Myra," he said. "She knows about her. They say she's very good."

O'Mara asked: "What about the husband?"

Guelvada spread his hands. "You know . . ." he said. "It was what you call 'one of those things'—an arranged marriage. De Sarieux was younger than she—about three or four years, I think, and he had a lot of wrong ideas."

"What wrong ideas?" asked O'Mara. He had finished tying the tie; stood back from the pier glass, examining the picture he presented.

"Wrong ideas about women, and drinking and cards and money, and also about Madame la Comtesse de Sarieux," said, Guelvada. "But definitely he had the wrong ideas about her. The marriage was not successful. It was one of those affairs which, in no circumstances, by no stretch of imagination, *could* have been successful. I think that she must have been very bored."

O'Mara fumbled in the bottom of the airplane kitbag that had held his new clothes. He produced a cigar box. He looked at it; opened it; smiled. Fifty of the small black South American cigars that he loved looked up at him from the box. He took one out, pierced it with a nail-file; lit it. He drew the smooth smoke down into his lungs.

He wondered about the cigars. He supposed that Tanga had asked Eleanor Frayne what sort of thing he smoked. She had found out somehow. Definitely, he thought, as Guelvada had said, she had an eye and a memory for detail.

He said: "And then?"

Guelvada shrugged his shoulders. "She didn't divorce him," he said, flickering the ash from his cigarette, "because he was a Catholic, and his family—who were nice people—did not like the idea. So it went on and the war came."

"And he got himself killed?" said O'Mara.

Guelvada shook his head. "He wasn't fit enough to join the Army or any of the Services," he said. "But she went to work on him after it seemed that France *must* be defeated. She managed to inspire him with a great deal of ardour—which was amazing.

He joined one of the first Resistance groups. They got him, and he died—not very pleasantly, I believe—at Dachau."

O'Mara asked: "What was she doing?"

"She's been working for Quayle ever since she saw that her marriage was a failure; ever since she realised that she did not really like de Sarieux," Guelvada answered. He stretched lazily.

"I like to watch her," he said. "I like to watch her walk. She walks with great grace and her voice is musical. She has taste and she is beautiful and has a peculiar quality of allure." He yawned. "She is very nice. And I am sorry that I do not know the English language to describe her better."

O'Mara grinned. He said: "You aren't doing so badly. What have you been at beside watching the Countess?"

"I have been talking to the maid Yvette," said Guelvada. "She also was unfortunate. Her husband was done by the Germans too. She is annoyed about that, because, apparently, she only began to realise his virtues *after* he was dead. It is a habit with women," he added.

He yawned again. "I have also been reading an old copy of *The Observer*—the English newspaper. I read in an article that in 1941 a Greek Minister 'caused confusion' when the Germans attacked by sending the whole of the Greek Army on leave. I thought that was very *naive*. And the words 'caused confusion' appealed to me greatly. I think that the English have a great capacity for understatement."

There was a long silence. O'Mara walked slowly about the room, trying his foot. He was feeling better. His burned fingers were less troublesome. He was keen to get to work.

He said: "About Ernestine."

Guelvada said: "She is very nice, my Ernestine. I like her. She is a great actress. She never stops acting and *anything* is grist to her histrionic mill. Even when her lover is pushed over a cliff she dramatises the situation. And in a very big way. Ernestine should be in Hollywood. She would do superbly . . . in glorious Technicolour."

"After you went down and saw what was left of Taudrille with her," said O'Mara. "After she'd seen the photograph and record which you had left on the body?"

"We climbed back to the cliff top," said Guelvada. "She proposed to take her bicycle and ride back to Saint Lys. I said that I could not hear of it. I said that I would put her bicycle on the back of the Typhoon and drive her over. She demurred at first but she really rather liked the idea."

He fingered his brown figured silk tie delicately.

"I think she goes for me," he said. "I think that in spite of her love for the late Taudrille she is slightly interested in Ernest Guelvada—possibly because she believes he was a friend of her late lover, but also a little because of himself. I went out for that."

"We'll take that for granted," said O'Mara. "What then?"

"I drove her back to Saint Lys," said Guelvada. "It was a nice drive. She told me all about herself and the man she thought was Taudrille. What a patriot he was! What a hero he was! I wanted to laugh. When we got to Saint Lys she directed me to a charming cottage about half a mile from the little wood behind the *depot* where, I imagine, the body of our friend Nago is still lying. This, she informed me, was her cottage where Taudrille used to visit her. I think that he was no fool."

"He had brains enough," said O'Mara.

"She asked me if I would like coffee and I said yes. We went inside. The place was quite charming and well furnished. She made coffee in the kitchen and I helped her. It was quite delightful. She told me how she had met Taudrille and how she had begun to love him because of his dangerous work for France. She said he was very kind to her and took a great interest in her work."

"I bet he did," said O'Mara. "Taudrille was clever enough to realise that this girl gave him a background in Saint Lys and the district. I expect he used her as a stooge, and the girl never guessed what he was doing."

"I think you are right," said Guelvada. "However . . . that is how it was. We drank coffee and it was very late and she told me about the theatre, and I have arranged to go and see her in a play to-night. She acts in a little theatre in Saint Lys. She belongs to a

Repertory Company. You know the sort of thing. She is playing an important part to-night and I have promised to give her an analytical criticism."

He smiled at O'Mara. "Then I said I must leave her and we had a dramatic parting. I told her that because she was Taudrille's friend she was also mine, and that just as Taudrille died for France so would I die for her if need be. It was all most dramatic and exciting," he continued. "Then she came to me and said that she trusted me and that she would be grateful if I would collect Taudrille's car and drive it to his cottage near Gouarec and put it in the garage. She gave me the key of the garage which Taudrille had left with her. And the address of the cottage."

"Nice work, Ernest," said O'Mara. "And then?"

"Then we embraced even more dramatically and I returned here."

O'Mara stopped walking about the room. He said: "The local *Maquis* leader here is a photographer named Jean Marie Larue, at 13 Rue des Pêcheurs, at Gouarec. You'd better get a hired car from somewhere—not here—and go over and see him before you go to Saint Lys to-night. Tell him to come here to-morrow night at about ten o'clock. I want to have a talk with him. He may know *something*—although I doubt it. Then carry on with Ernestine. By the way, what's her other name?"

"At the theatre," said Guelvada, "she calls herself Ernestine Duvallier. But her real name is Ernestine Rumianska. Her father was a Pole and her mother a school teacher of Nantes. Her father, whom she adored, commanded a battalion of Russian infantry. He died in a prisoner-of-war camp. That is why she does not like the Nazis. Her mother, whom she has not seen for years, she dislikes very much. It was because of her mother's bad temper that the father returned to Russia."

"I see," said O'Mara. "Well, work on her. Get into her confidence. Taudrille may have told her *something,* and even if we only discover lies it may help somehow."

"It is often very useful to discover lies," said Guelvada. "Also it is very interesting to know that she was responsible for getting Nago to Saint Lys. She was quite frank about it."

"What did she say?" O'Mara sat on the bed and regarded Guelvada intently.

"Taudrille told her he was going to Saint Lys on very secret and important business," said Guelvada. "He told her that an associate of his named Nago would be on the Saint Brieuc-Saint Lys road between certain times. He asked her if she could arrange to get him a lift to Saint Lys. She did so. Apparently she is friendly with a tradesman who collects fish catches from the coast centres in the evening. It was arranged that this man was to pick up Nago at a road inter-section, where he would be waiting for the fish van. Nago was picked up and was, apparently, dropped somewhere near the *depot* at Saint Lys. She knew this because, when Taudrille did not appear, she thought that possibly he might have sent her a note by the van driver. So she asked him and he told her about Nago."

O'Mara said: "I see." He thought that the jig-saw puzzle was beginning to sort itself out. Jig-saw puzzles always did sort themselves out—if you waited long enough.

He went over to the window; stood by Guelvada, looking out on to the grounds.

The Typhoon came round the house; proceeded slowly along the drive to the main entrance gates. The sun shone on the polished car.

O'Mara watched Tanga's hands as, white-gloved, they rested easily on the wheel.

Guelvada said: "I put a lot of work in on that car. I cleaned it beautifully, as you will see. I did not know that there was a man who did that."

"What man?" asked O'Mara.

"He is called Desart," said Guelvada. "He does odd jobs and helps the gardener. He is a nice old man with white hair. He likes to talk. And he is most amusing."

He lit a cigarette. "Are you feeling better?" he asked.

"I'm all right," said O'Mara. "Now that I've stopped drinking that rot-gut of Volanon's. And you'd better be moving, Ernest. Take one of the afternoon buses to Coulan and walk from there to the church on the Saint Brieuc estuary—it isn't far. Pick up Taudrille's car and take it back to his garage. Put the car in the garage and lock it; then, when you see Ernestine to-night, tell her you have garaged it and return the key to her. Meet her after the theatre to-night; talk her into asking you back to her cottage or give her supper or something, but keep her busy until one or two in the morning."

"I see," said Guelvada. He smiled. "It should not be difficult," he said. "Taudrille's cottage is about twelve miles from Saint Lys—on the main Gouarec-Saint Brieuc road. Would you like me to take a look at it?"

"No," said O'Mara. "Just leave the car in the garage."

Guelvada got up. He picked up his soft felt hat from the table. He said: "I am glad to see you looking so much better."

"Thanks," said O'Mara. He smiled at Guelvada. He said: "There's nothing like work to make a sick man well."

"Yes," said Guelvada. He took the Swedish knife from the crown of his hat, pressed the spring. The blade shot out. He ran a finger delicately along the edge. He replaced the knife in the hat.

He said: "There is nothing like work. I'll be seeing you."

He went out.

O'Mara finished his small cigar; put the stub in the tray; went down the stairs into the grounds at the back of the house. After a little while he found the man Desart at work in the gardener's shed. Desart was sixty, thin, and voluble. He had a face like a wrinkled apple and a perpetual grin which showed his lack of teeth.

O'Mara gave him a cigarette. Then he leaned against the doorpost of the shed and began to talk.

It was nearly ten o'clock. O'Mara, at one end of the table, smoked one of his small cigars; regarded Tanga de Sarieux, who sat at the other end, with an amiable eye.

He said: "I think it was nice of somebody to think about these cigars. Did Eleanor Frayne tell you?"

She said: "Yes, I asked her; then I spoke to M'sieu Varin in Paris. He said he could get some."

He said: "You think of everything."

She said demurely: "I try to be kind."

"And how you succeed," said O'Mara. "And all this is quite charming. An excellent dinner in delightful surroundings; a kind and beautiful hostess. I was thinking . . ."

He stopped in the middle of the sentence.

"What were you thinking?" she asked. "Or was it something that you had decided was not for my ears?"

"I was thinking that life like this might be very good," said O'Mara. "I think the atmosphere is very fascinating."

She said: "You overwhelm me." She flashed one of her sudden smiles at him. "May I say that your clothes look very nice?"

"Thanks to you," said O'Mara. He thought to himself that they were beginning to sound like a mutual admiration society. He went on: "I have usually found that women who are as beautiful as you are seldom good organisers. *You* are even good at that." He grinned at her through the cigar smoke.

She said: "That was a charming speech, O'Mara. Did you rehearse it?"

He shook his head. He asked: "Why?"

She began to peel a peach. "It *might* have been rehearsed," she said. She cut the peach, put a slice into her mouth. He watched her. He found the process fascinating.

"It might have been rehearsed, because that is how you sound sometimes when you talk to me—just as if you had rehearsed it first. I know why. . . ."

O'Mara raised his eyebrows. "Really?" he said. "Then tell *me* why."

She put another piece of peach in her mouth. She ate it slowly, looking at him. There was a mischievous twinkle in her eye.

She said: "You are rather afraid to let yourself go, aren't you, O'Mara? You find yourself at dinner with a woman who—I am glad to say—you do not find positively unattractive or boring. You can do one of two things. You can do this or do that. You can be careful or audacious. Because you are being careful, you are also careful in what you say. You content yourself with paying compliments. You think that is the *safe* thing. Is it not so, O'Mara?"

He smiled at her. "You miss very little," he said. "And if what you say is true—and I don't admit it—perhaps you can tell me why."

She said: "It *is* true whether you admit it or not. It is true and the reason is this. It is because you think it would not be clever for you to say anything to me that might create a situation between us which could possibly affect either your own or my efficiency in the work we are doing. You are worried about that work. I imagine that it does not go well and you are in what the Americans call 'a spot.'"

O'Mara was still smiling. He said: "So I'm in a spot?"

"I think so," she answered. "You are worried. First of all, you are not completely fit. Your hand is still bad. You are already wondering just how you are going to deal with the situation that confronts you. You know that Quayle expects you to deal with it. You are thinking of your reputation."

"Why not?" asked O'Mara.

She shrugged her shoulders. "Why not?" she said softly. "You have a reputation for being clever and completely ruthless. You would be quite ruthless—even with yourself; just as Quayle was ruthless with you. Those two who burned your hand might just as easily have killed you. . . ."

"All right," said O'Mara. "Let's take all that for granted. Well . . ."

"You would be just as tough, as ruthless, with me as Quayle would be with you; as you would be with yourself—*if* the situation demanded it. You are thinking that possibly the situation *will* demand it, and so you have decided that it is better, for the moment, to keep me at arm's length with compliments, rather than risk disturbing my mentality, and what you call 'the atmosphere,' by any other approach. You need not worry." She smiled again. "I am quite ready to be sacrificed."

O'Mara thought: Here's a damned clever woman. With brains as well as beauty.

He said: "Nuts!" He grinned at her.

"You know that what I say is true," she said. "But tell me, what happens now? Am I permitted to know what is going on?"

O'Mara said: "Nothing's going on at the moment, and I think you're doing very well. I have no complaints."

She said: "Precisely. But up to the moment my activities have been somewhat limited, have they not? A few telephone calls to London; to M'sieu Varin in Paris; some domestic arrangements which are very easy because the de Chervasses did all that for me. But none of this is very difficult or very important."

She took a cigarette from the silver box on the table. O'Mara got up, lit it for her.

"Mr. Quayle often found much more interesting things for me to do," she added.

O'Mara said: "I don't doubt that."

She said: "I consider it to be most unsatisfactory. Will you have some more coffee?"

O'Mara said: "No, thank you." He went on: "I shall be out to-night. I might be late. Ernest Guelvada will certainly be late. If I were you I should take the opportunity of getting a good night's sleep."

She said: "You said that before, this morning. I always sleep well. I'm not at all tired." She added: "I expect I shall be up when you return." She laughed. "I hope, in addition to coffee, I shall not have to stand by with the first-aid case—not this time."

O'Mara said seriously: "I sincerely hope you won't."

There was silence for a moment; then she asked: "Don't you think it would be foolish of you to walk into any unnecessary trouble at this time before you are quite fit?"

O'Mara said: "I never walk into *unnecessary* trouble. And there's nothing" very much the matter with me now. But it was nice of you to think about it."

She said: "Not at all. It was quite normal." She leaned her elbows on the table. She said: "I wonder why you spend most of your time fencing with me."

O'Mara cocked one eyebrow. "Was I?" he asked.

She said: "Yes. You are a little diffident in your conversation—a little trite." She smiled. "It is quite unnecessary for you to be afraid of me."

O'Mara laughed. "Now you're being quite amusing," he said. "Will you tell me why I should be afraid of you, as you call it?"

She said: "Perhaps 'afraid' is the wrong word. I do not know the word in English that I want."

"It doesn't matter," said O'Mara. "Let's call the word 'afraid.' Why should I be afraid of you?"

She said: "I don't know. Possibly because Eulalia was a friend of mine and she talked to me about you."

O'Mara said: "Oh . . . that . . .! Why should I be afraid of that?"

"Of course there is no reason at all. I should not have used the word 'afraid.'" She leaned forward. "Tell me," she said, "did you find her very charming—very delightful?"

O'Mara felt vaguely uncomfortable. He said: "You're perfectly right. The word wasn't 'afraid.' The word was 'uncomfortable.'"

"Of course," she said. "That's the word I wanted. Sometimes talking to me makes you slightly uncomfortable." She smiled again. He saw the flash of her white teeth. She repeated: "Was she delightful and amusing as well as beautiful? And did she know what your work in Rio was—before you met her?"

He said: "She was delightful and amusing as well as beautiful. Naturally, she knew nothing of my work. Why should she?" He added brusquely: "Any more questions?"

She shook her dark head. She said: "No. Now I think you are being somewhat like a pig again."

He said: "There are moments when I like to be somewhat like a pig." He changed the subject. "Tell me what happened this afternoon. Did you see Volanon? Ernest Guelvada and I watched you from my bedroom window as you were driving away."

She said: "How nice of you both. Yes, I went to the *Garage Volanon* and talked with him. He was leaning against the garage door. He looked as if he had been drinking a little, and he was smoking a fearful cigarette. Its odour was terrible."

O'Mara said: "Yes." He could visualise the scene.

"I asked him if it would be convenient to do the work that I had wanted done on the car—the work I had spoken about with his assistant. He looked surprised. He said he did not know what I meant."

O'Mara asked: "What happened then?"

She said: "I told him that when I came to the garage the other day I had asked Garenne, his assistant, if it would be possible to have the engine of the Typhoon cleaned. I told him that Garenne had said yes; that if I brought the car back one afternoon early—about three o'clock—he would do it."

O'Mara asked: "What did Volanon say to that?"

She said: "He told me Garenne had gone. He said that Garenne was a drunken sot and no good; that he was entirely without character. He also said that in his more sober moments Garenne was given to chasing women in the village; that on the other hand he might be sleeping off a fit of alcoholic stupor. I pretended to be quite shocked at this. I asked him why he did not get a more sober assistant; that I should have thought there were young men in the neighbourhood who would have been glad to have found work. He took quite a time to reply to that. Then he said that, in spite of his faults, Garenne suited him. When he was sober he worked quite well, and that he understood a man not being sober."

O'Mara said: "I didn't know he was so human. What did you say to that one?"

She said: "I told him that I thought it was extremely bad to employ people who were drunk most of the time, to which he replied that there was usually a reason for a man drinking; that he imagined you had some sort of secret sorrow; that he thought you were trying to forget a woman or something." She looked at him archly. "Were you?" she said.

O'Mara laughed. "I don't have to get drunk to forget women," he said.

She said: "No?"

"Did he say anything else?" asked O'Mara.

"No," she answered. "Nothing else. He said that it was possible that Garenne would return in a day or so. He said that often when you had had a very bad attack of alcohol you would go up to the church and walk about the yew-tree grove. He said you had been known to sleep there for days. Once, he said, you slept there through a rainstorm. You were discovered with your head resting on a tombstone. Life must have been very uncomfortable for you."

"It was," said O'Mara. "So, boiled down to hard facts, Volanon is not at all perturbed at my absence. He thinks I am either getting over a drunk, or having got over a drunk am chasing some of the women of the town. Well, it's quite normal for him to think that, I suppose. Both those things have happened before—at least before I began to get too drunk permanently. Thank you very much."

She said: "I hope you have the information you wanted." She got up from the table. She said: "Now I shall read. I hope you have a very interesting and successful evening."

"I hope so too," said O'Mara. He held the door open for her. He said: "I'd like to use the Typhoon to-night. I take it that you won't be needing a car."

She looked at him with wide eyes. She said: "But of course not. I shall be waiting, like a good hostess, for the return of my guests. And I shall not even be inquisitive."

O'Mara looked at her. One quick glance took in the soft dinner blouse of white lace with its heart-shaped front caught with a diamond brooch; the long slim black marocain skirt, slit to the calf, that showed small diamond-buckled black satin shoes and a glimpse of a slender ankle.

He said: "Not only beautiful but of great perception." His smile was embracing.

She returned the smile. "Two essentially feminine qualities which, up to the moment, seem to have been wasted on desert air. *Au revoir,* O'Mara."

He closed the door behind her; returned to the table; poured himself a small glass of brandy; drank it. He went through the open french windows on to the lawn at the back of the house. He walked across the lawn; stood looking down over the hill towards the Saint Brieuc estuary, where the lights were already twinkling. On the left he could just make out the lighted window of the *Café Volanon,* and next to it the upper room, Volanon's room, in the garage. There was a light in that too.

He began to walk along the gravelled path on the far side of the lawn. The path ran over the hill, between trees and shrubs. There was a pleasant air of mystery about the place which might, at some other time, have been very attractive. So O'Mara thought.

It was dark amongst the trees. Over the sea there was a good moon. O'Mara looked at his wrist-watch; saw that it was half-past eleven.

He began to think of Desart—the old man who helped the gardener at the Villa—who had been so surprised—after he had recognised O'Mara—to realise that Garenne—the lately drunken assistant at the *Garage Volanon*—was now a guest of Madame la Comtesse de Sarieux at the *Villa Cote d'Azur*.

That, thought O'Mara, was going to be too much for Desart. By now he would have unfolded the story to a group of wide-open ears at the *Nouveau Café*—his own particular stamping ground in the fishing quarter at Saint Brieuc. By now the story would be on its rounds. O'Mara wondered if Volanon had heard it yet.

The night was warm; ideal for driving. O'Mara walked back to the lawn, crossed it, went to the garage on the east side of the house and opened the doors. He started up the Typhoon, backed the car out, closed the doors and stood leaning against the car whilst the engine warmed up. He was thinking about Rozanski; wondering where he was, what he was doing; how much he knew about the set-up in Saint Brieuc.

He must know a great deal. Rozanski's contacts had been quick to act on the information that had been "extracted" from O'Mara by Morosc and Nago. Within a matter of hours the unfortunate new tenant of Quayle's offices in Pall Mall had been shot—in mistake for Quayle. Rozanski was well organised—up to a point.

He got into the car; drove slowly down the drive, through the back gates. He turned to the left and made for the woods above Gourant Farm. The car ran smoothly, and O'Mara, who had not driven a car for many months, was glad to find that he was at home behind the wheel.

He swung left again on the hilltop behind the farm, took a secondary road for three miles, then swung to the right and drove on to the main Quimper-Gouarec road that passed behind Saint Brieuc village and from which a subsidiary road led off towards the church and the yew-tree grove on the far side of the Saint Brieuc estuary.

The road stretched before O'Mara, silvered in the moonlight, shadowed here and there by the groups of tall trees. He put his foot down on the accelerator, saw the speedometer mount up over sixty miles an hour.

He sat behind the wheel, the wind blowing through his hair, enjoying the speed. He kept the car between fifty and seventy miles an hour for nearly ten miles, decelerating only slightly for the wide curves; taking the sharper turns on the brakes.

Then he slowed down. He stopped the car in a patch of shadow, fumbled in his pocket for one of the small cigars. He lit it, sat enjoying the night, congratulating himself that nearly ten months of bad liquor and a worse diet had not affected his driving nerve.

He restarted the car. Two miles farther he took the left fork on to the subsidiary road. Now he was running downhill. Saint Brieuc lay beneath and behind him, and the road narrowed until, six or seven miles ahead, it joined the dirt road that ran past the church.

He increased speed; then decreased as he saw a mile or so ahead of him a light. The light seemed to be somewhere on the cliff edge. O'Mara slowed down to thirty miles an hour, stopped the car apposite the light, got out and walked over the grass verge towards the solitary figure that stood by the lantern on the cliff edge.

The policeman—it was one of the Saint Lys rural *gendarmerie*—moved towards him.

"Is there some trouble?" asked O'Mara. "Can I do anything?"

The policeman shook his head. "You are too late, M'sieu," he said. "One has decided to fall over the cliff—or to be pushed." He shrugged his shoulders. "There is nothing to be done about it—except the morgue."

O'Mara asked: "A local person?"

"No one knows," said the policeman. "The Chief of Police from Saint Lys has been here and made the search himself." He grinned at O'Mara. "He did not do me the honour of discussing the matter with me. They propose to move it in the morning."

O'Mara said: "It's a long way to fall. Well . . . good night."

So that was that. Varien had instructed the Saint Lys police, and Taudrille's body was "discovered." O'Mara thought that things might begin to move. It was time things moved.

He went back to the car; drove past the church on to the Gouarec road, then, fifteen miles farther on, by-passing Gouarec, turned on to the main Saint Lys road. At the inter-section about eight miles from Saint Lys he parked the car on the grass verge and began to walk. Fifteen minutes' walking brought him to Taudrille's cottage.

The cottage, with its white walls and red roof, made an attractive picture in the moonlight. It stood back from the deserted road, in a well-kept lawn surrounded by a low white wall, with a gate at the end.

O'Mara went through the gate, followed the well-kept path round the right-hand side of the house, stopped at the back door. A few yards away was the garage, reached from the side road, and O'Mara could see the fresh tracks of the tyres on the gravel where Guelvada had driven the car in.

There was a window with wire netting a few feet from the door. O'Mara examined it. It was not fastened. He opened it, got through, closed it behind him. He was in a room which might have been used as a kitchen. O'Mara opened a door; found himself in the short passage which led from the back door to the front entrance. There was a room on the left simply furnished as a bedroom and the room in front—the sitting-room—ran the whole breadth of the small cottage.

There were lace curtains at the windows, but the moonlight illuminated the room, showed it to be better furnished than the bedroom. It was a clean, comfortable room with a settee, two arm-chairs—one each side of the fireplace—and a small book-case that seemed almost empty. The furniture was old-fashioned.

O'Mara looked at his wrist-watch. It was nearly one o'clock. He went back to the kitchen and began a systematic search—using Guelvada's pencil torch when it was necessary. He searched the kitchen, the bedroom; came back to the sitting-room and examined it closely. He realised that it was difficult to look for something of which you were not aware.

He stood in front of the bookcase, looking at the two books which occupied its otherwise bare shelves. O'Mara took out one of the books. It was a *Life* of *Napoleon* by Charles Duroc. It was an old book, well bound and printed on good paper. Most of the leaves were uncut. O'Mara replaced the *Life of Napoleon*; took up the other book. It was a translation into Polish of Shakespeare's Plays done by Julian Korsak in Vilna in 1840.

O'Mara carried it to the table in his right hand; held it spine downwards on the table, holding the covers together with his fingers. He took his hand away. The book opened at pages 410-411. The pages were printed in good type and were clean except in one place where a smudge showed.

He took the book to the corner of the room farthest from the window; stood with his back to the light; examined the pages with his small flash. Two lines of the print had been underlined in pencil and someone had taken the trouble to erase the pencil marks, leaving a smudge from a not-too-clean eraser.

O'Mara read the lines that had been marked:

> *"Co po imieniu? Roza choc nazwisko mieni*
> *Czyliz sie, mniej powabnym kolorem rumieni."*

O'Mara translated the words into English. He wondered if Julian Korsak had decided to improve on Shakespeare, for his words put back into English were:

> *"What's in a name? The rose its title altered*
> *Still crimsons for me with enchanting colour."*

O'Mara thought he preferred Shakespeare's original:

> *"What's in a name? That which we call a rose*
> *By any other name would smell as sweet."*

But he did not see why he should worry about it. Perhaps the Korsak translation was prettier if you liked it that way.

He shrugged his shoulders. He shut the book; crossed the room; replaced it in the bookcase. He thought that Taudrille must have had little time for reading; that in any case his tastes must have been peculiar to have existed on the *Life of Napoleon* and William Shakespeare's Plays in Polish.

O'Mara moved to the centre of the room. He took his last cigar from his pocket and bit the end off. He felt vaguely disappointed.

Although he had considered the searching of Taudrille's cottage to be more or less of a routine affair, yet he had hoped that *something* might be there. Something in the atmosphere; some *thing* that would suggest a line of thought or action.

He realised that this cottage must have played an important part in the plans of Taudrille and more importantly in the plans of the man behind Taudrille, the man who desired above all things to kill Quayle, the Nazi who called himself Rozanski. This cottage was situated roughly in the centre of the area round Gouarec where Quayle's last four agents had met their deaths. It should have had a tale to tell and it told nothing. Nothing at all.

O'Mara was impatient. He had a reputation for speed; for luck; for toughness. He knew this. He knew that Quayle had thought that these three qualities might make for success on a job that was not easy. O'Mara thought that possibly he had been in too much of a hurry about Taudrille. Maybe Taudrille would have been worth more alive than dead.

If it had been possible to keep him alive.

He shrugged his shoulders. He took his lighter from his pocket and lit the cigar. There was nothing more for him to do. He turned towards the doorway. He stopped as he saw the door opening.

Volanon stood in the doorway. His face was dark with rage; greasy with sweat. His stomach sagged over the top of his filthy blue linen trousers. He presented a formidable picture. O'Mara realised that he was not even drunk. The brown hand that held the automatic pistol was quite steady.

The two men stood looking at each other. Volanon was trying to speak. O'Mara realised that the Frenchman was almost strangled with rage. He drew on his cigar. He thought it would be very tough to be shot for inadequate reasons in a deserted cottage by an infuriated Frenchman. Volanon found words:

He said: "Filthy son of a pig . . . lousy murdering swine . . .! So you thought you could delude Papa Volanon. I am going to kill you, Garenne."

He took a step forward into the room. The hand holding the pistol moved up.

O'Mara said: "Don't be a damned fool, Volanon; that is, don't be a greater imbecile than fate has already made you. The trouble with you is you drink too much and your mind—or lack of it—runs away with you. Why don't you relax?"

Volanon said: "So you will try and talk yourself out of this, but you will not do it. I am going to execute you. I shall like doing that."

O'Mara said: "You may like doing that, but you won't like being guillotined for it."

Volanon began to laugh. He said: "Do not be a fool. Do you really think I shall be guillotined for killing you? Surely you have been in this part of the world long enough to know that the Maquis are cleaning up traitors when they find them? Do you think that the police are going to be very angry with me; to want to guillotine me; when they know about you?" Volanon stopped for breath. "You lousy filthy traitor," he said. "You are talking to Emil Volanon, who worked with the *Maquis*. You are talking to a man who helped the British fliers to get back to England during the war. You are talking to a man who helped British and French Agents. Everyone who came to this part of the world who was against the Nazis was helped by Papa Volanon." He laughed. "Your body will be found here. The police will know who and what you were. My friends—everyone—will congratulate me on having killed you."

O'Mara said: "Yes? And exactly what do you mean by the police knowing who I was? I told you not to be an imbecile, Volanon. I repeat the advice."

O'Mara put his hands in his trouser pockets; regarded the Frenchman with equanimity.

Volanon said: "You killed a good Frenchman. You murdered Taudrille. They found his body to-night. He had been pushed over the cliff not far from the church; not far from the yew-tree grove where you used to go in your more drunken moments. I thought you were sleeping off your liquor. Now I know that you were plotting—probably meeting with your friends, the remnants of that filthy crowd of Nazi spies, Werewolves, riffraff, who tried to carry on the tradition of Hitler even after he is dead, and after his associates have paid the price. You killed Taudrille."

O'Mara said: "All right. I killed Taudrille if you like. But things are not always what they seem, Volanon. It would not be good for you if you made a mistake. It would go very hard with you if you killed someone who was found to be a friend of France."

Volanon said in his thick voice: "You—a friend of France. . . . Hear me laugh. Now I am going to kill you."

O'Mara said: "You might like to wait a minute before you do it. There are two things I'd like to point out to you. You say you've worked with the *Maquis* here; that you've helped the British. That ought to make you think. When you were working with the *Maquis* when France was occupied, did you not hear of cases of men who seemed to be working with the Germans who were really working for France? Of course you did. And how do you know about Taudrille? They are saying, I suppose, that Taudrille was a good Frenchman. Why are they saying that? I'll tell you. They are saying it because they found in a pocket on his body a photograph of himself and his record in the Second Bureau, in the *Maquis* and the French Army. How do I know that?" O'Mara grinned. "Because I put it there. If I had killed Taudrille, do you think I should have been foolish enough to have left that photograph on him? Another thing—supposing the person they found at the foot of the cliff was not Taudrille; supposing it was someone else?"

Volanon said: "Why should I listen to you?"

O'Mara detected a note of doubt in his voice. He said: "I don't know why you should listen, but you are listening."

Volanon said: "You told me there were two reasons why I should not kill you. You have told me the first. I do not think it is a very good one, but I will hear the second. I like to satisfy my curiosity."

He came a little closer. The automatic pistol was pointing at O'Mara's chest.

O'Mara said: "I'll give you the second reason. That's a very old gun you're using." He looked at the automatic. He saw that the safety-catch was off. He saw that all Volanon had to do was to squeeze the trigger. He took a chance. He said: "You're not very used to firearms, are you, Volanon—in spite of your service with the *Maquis?* The safety-catch of that pistol is on. It's going to take you a couple of seconds to move your thumb and push it off. You should have thought of that."

Volanon did what O'Mara thought he would do. He looked down at the pistol.

At that moment, O'Mara sprang. He knocked the hand holding the pistol up with his knee; gave Volanon a vicious short-arm jab on the side of the jaw. The automatic fired a bullet into the ceiling. Volanon described a small arc; finished up on the floor, his head banging against the door. O'Mara put his left foot on the automatic pistol, which was still in Volanon's right hand.

He said: "Let go of that gun or I'll kick your teeth in."

Volanon released the pistol. O'Mara moved it away with his foot; bent down; picked it up gingerly with his injured hand. He put it in his pocket.

He said: "I'll add that to the collection I've got at home in England. Now, Papa, sit down in that arm-chair and relax. I'm going to talk a little sense to you."

Volanon got up. He fingered his jaw tenderly. His eyes still blazed with anger. O'Mara thought, in parentheses, that Papa Volanon wasn't such a bad type after all; in spite of the bad drink, the bad wages and the bad food, he was still—like most Bretons—a good Frenchman.

Volanon sat down in the arm-chair. His eyes never left O'Mara's. O'Mara stood in front of the fireplace, his hands in his trouser pockets.

He said: "Listen, Papa. . . . If I were the man you took me to be, if I were the man who had killed Taudrille because he was a friend of France, quite obviously I should kill you, even if only for the purpose of stopping your mouth. The fact that I don't intend to do so should prove something to you."

Volanon said nothing.

O'Mara went on: "In a minute you're going to get out of here. By the way, how did you get here?"

"How do I get anywhere?" said Volanon. "I got here on my bicycle."

"Where is it?" asked O'Mara.

Volanon said: "I hid it behind the garage under a bush where no one could see it."

O'Mara thought for a moment. He said: "All right. Well, you can ride it back to the garage. When you get there I should open up a bottle of that bad brandy of yours; give yourself a good drink and ask yourself a few questions. If you do that, you'll find you'll be a lot easier in your mind."

"Yes," said Volanon in a surly tone. "What questions?"

"First of all," said O'Mara, "ask yourself why I should have killed Taudrille and not killed you, if I am what you think I am. Secondly, you will ask yourself if there might not possibly be a connection between an individual whom I think is known to you—one Jean Marie Larue, who lives at 13 Rue Pêcheurs, Gouarec?"

O'Mara looked at Volanon. He said: "Does that mean anything to you?"

Volanon said: *"Mon Dieu* . . . you know Jean? Does he know you?"

"No," said O'Mara. "He doesn't. Not yet, but I know him." He went on: "You heard that I was staying at the *Villa Cote d'Azur*—a guest of the lady who brought the Typhoon car down to the garage a few days ago to have a puncture repaired. You thought that was very strange. You thought it an amazing thing that your drunken assistant—Philippe Garenne—should be staying at the Villa as a guest of that lady, and you thought some other things too. You heard some other things. Then you heard that Taudrille's body had been discovered, and you decided to finish me off. You thought that would be a good thing to do. You thought the *Maquis* would be very pleased with you." He grinned. "You thought that would not be the first traitor who had disappeared in this area since the Liberation."

O'Mara drew on his cigar. "Papa, you have been wrong from the start. To-morrow, Jean Marie Larue will come to see me at the *Villa Cote d'Azur*. That fact in itself should tell you all you want to know."

Volanon said in a quiet voice: "Philippe, you are trying to tell me that . . ."

"I'm not trying to tell you anything," said O'Mara. "I'm telling you that the man you thought was Taudrille was a Nazi. I killed him. I like killing Nazis. If you like to speak to Jean Larue the day after to-morrow he will confirm what I say." O'Mara smiled. "If he doesn't, you will still find me at the Villa. You can come along and bring your pistol with you. But you won't."

Volanon said: "I am not sure about you, Philippe. I am not quite certain."

O'Mara said: "I understand that. But you will be. Now go and get your bicycle and go back to the *Garage Volanon*."

Volanon got to his feet. He spread his hands in a gesture of resignation. He said: "What can I do?"

"Exactly," said O'Mara. "You'd much better do what I tell you. There is one other thing: if you are a good Frenchman, Papa, you're going to keep your mouth shut. I'm not asking you to keep your mouth shut. I'm telling you to. If you speak you will be an enemy of France."

Volanon said with an air of dignity which made him look rather absurd: "I shall speak to no one. I shall wait until the day after to-morrow. I shall ride my bicycle to Gouarec. I shall see Jean Larue. If he confirms what you say, all well and good. If not, I shall find you."

O'Mara said: "That's a bet, Papa. Good night." He took the pistol out of his pocket. "Here's your gun," he said. "You may still have a chance to use it on some odd Nazi. But next time find a real one."

Volanon put the pistol in his pocket. He said: "Philippe, I am almost beginning to believe in you. It would be strange if I had had an Englishman working in my garage for all these months and not known it. It would be very strange."

He went to the door. He looked over his shoulder. He said: "But I tell you, if Jean Larue does not confirm what you say we shall get you."

O'Mara said: "All right."

Volanon went away.

Two minutes afterwards, from the window, O'Mara saw him ride away. He waited ten minutes: then he left the cottage by the back window; walked down the road; got into the Typhoon; drove towards Saint Brieuc. He took the by-pass road that led across the hill that flanked the estuary. He drove at a moderate speed, thinking about all sorts of things, but mainly concerned with Volanon.

It was a quarter-past two when he swung the car round the sharp bend by the clump of trees on to the road that led past the back entrance to the Villa. He checked the car still more as he turned into the open gateway. As he did so, there was a sharp sound. The windshield in front of him shattered.

O'Mara drove the car through the gates; stopped; jumped over the side; waited. He could hear faintly the sound of running foot-steps. He waited two or three minutes; then he got into the car; drove it up the drive into the garage. He locked the garage doors.

He put his hand to his face. When he brought it away there was blood on it. A splinter from the shattered windshield had torn open his cheek. He cursed to himself. He went round to the front of the house; rang the door-bell. He waited. After a minute the door opened. Yvette stood in the hallway.

She said: *"Mon Dieu* . . . Monsieur O'Mara . . . always when you come here you are hurt. I am beginning to think that you have what motorists call an accident complex."

Tanga appeared at the head of the stairs leading from the hallway.

She said: "Good morning, O'Mara. I promised that I would have coffee ready for you. It seems that you also need medical attention." She came down the stairs. She said: "Yvette, get the medical case."

Yvette went away.

Tanga asked: "What happened? Is it bad?"

O'Mara shook his head. "A scratch," he said. "Somebody put a bullet through the windshield just as I was coming into the drive."

She shrugged her shoulders. She said: "One is beginning to believe that you are not very popular in these parts. But you had better come and sit down whilst I do your face." She added in a sympathetic voice: "Once on a time you were quite good looking. By the time you have finished here, if you are not luckier, your face will be so disfigured that you will be beautifully unattractive. Lovely women will like to be seen out with you merely for the contrast."

O'Mara said: "That will be very nice, I am sure."

He followed her up the stairs.

Ten minutes afterwards he came out of Tanga's room. The adhesive tape on one side of his face made an extraordinary contrast to the bruise on the other side, acquired from Morosc, which was in process of disappearing. He walked along the passage towards his own room; saw the crack of light under the door of Guelvada's bedroom. O'Mara walked to the end of the passage; opened the door.

Guelvada was busy at the wash-basin. He was holding the blade of his small Swedish knife under the running faucet. O'Mara raised his eyebrows. He saw the colour of the water.

He asked: "Have you been using that?"

Guelvada turned his head; looked at O'Mara over his shoulder. His expression was almost beatific. He said: "Why not? I decided to take a little walk-to-night. I heard your car in the distance. I came back. I was not far from the gate when that person fired a shot at you. I saw you get out of the car. I knew you were all right."

O'Mara said: "Well?"

"I was behind a tree," Guelvada went on, "only six or seven yards from him when he fired. I was on him before he could fire a second shot. He was strong —that one—a young man too. It was quite interesting."

O'Mara said: "*How* interesting?"

Guelvada shrugged his shoulders. "We had a struggle," he said. "I think I hurt him a little; then he got away. I went after him. He ran for some distance; then he tripped up on a branch; fell over. I think that winded him, but he had time to get up and get his knife out."

Guelvada began to wipe the blade of his knife on a hand-towel. He said: "I looked at him and weighed up the situation. He was very much younger than I was. I thought it would be unfortunate and rather stupid for me to get hurt at this time."

"I see," said O'Mara grimly. "So you threw the knife?"

Guelvada said: "Yes. It was a beautiful shot in the throat—right in the centre of the artery at the side just under the Adam's apple."

O'Mara said: "Where is he?"

"I put him under some bushes," said Guelvada. "I should think it would be a long time before anyone found him."

O'Mara said: "This place is being draped with bodies. First Morosc, then Nago, then Taudrille. Now this one. I suppose you wouldn't know who he was?"

Guelvada shook his head.

O'Mara said: "Good night, Ernest."

He went back to his room.

Guelvada began to polish the blade of his knife.

CHAPTER FOUR
ROZANSKI

O'MARA and Guelvada walked up and down the wide lawn. It was eight o'clock; the shadows were lengthening; a breeze came over from the sea.

Guelvada said: "She is amusing and has a certain amount of brains—this little Ernestine. Last night, after the performance, it was all over the place in Saint Lys that a body had been found on the rocks near Saint Brieuc. That in itself would have caused little surprise. The discoveries of bodies in this part of the world during the last year is no new thing. The *Maquis* have long memories and long knives. But this case was different. It was said that the man was a French *agent*; one of the men who were searching for hidden Nazis in France. There was talk at the theatre. One of the dressers heard the news during an *entr'acte*. When the performance was over I met Ernestine. She was preoccupied. I could see that something was on her mind. She said that she had something to do. So I waited for her at a café in the town."

O'Mara said: "I suppose she went to the police."

Guelvada nodded. "She went to the police. She knows one of the sergeants. She discovered that they had found Nago's body; and the suicide note that was on it. She was able to tell me that the wording of the suicide note found on Nago was the same as the one she had found on Taudrille. She was certain that both Nago and Taudrille had been killed by the same person."

O'Mara asked: "Did she tell the police that?"

"No," said Guelvada. "She reserved the information for me. She said that now it would be easier for me to discover Taudrille's murderer. She said that it must have been someone who knew his plans; who knew where to find him and where to find Nago. She is filled with hatred for the murderer."

O'Mara said: "You'd better keep your eyes skinned where Ernestine is concerned. Has it struck you that she may still suspect *you* of having killed Taudrille and Nago? Maybe she's just playing you along."

Guelvada shrugged his shoulders. "There is always the chance," he said. "But I don't think so. I think she is quite charming and is finding a certain amount of drama in the situation. I think she is beginning to forget about Taudrille. . . ."

"You mean she's beginning to fall for *you*?" said O'Mara.

Guelvada said: "Other women have found such a process not difficult."

O'Mara asked: "What about Jean Larue?"

"He is coming here to-night," Guelvada replied. "At ten-thirty—when it is dark. He seems to be a good type. He is coming by bicycle via Gourant Farm so as not to be seen near Saint Brieuc. He will come into the Villa grounds by the side gate, cross the lawn in the shadow of the garden wall and knock at the french windows. He says there are more damned Nazis about this countryside than one thinks."

There was a silence. Then O'Mara said: "I'm worried about Ernestine. I think she'll do something soon. I think she's making up her mind. When she's had time to think about the strange coincidence of Nago's suicide note being the same as the one she found on Taudrille she may decide to do something about it. She may go to the police again."

Guelvada said: "She *had* that idea. I talked her out of it. I said that it might interfere with my work; that it might make things more difficult for me. I told her that I would think about it and that when I saw her to-night I would advise her."

O'Mara said: "You'd better play for time. When you see her to-night, tell her that you've been in touch with Headquarters in Paris; say that they're going to move in the matter. Arrange to see her to-morrow night, when you will be able to tell her more. Keep her quiet until then."

Guelvada nodded. "I can play her along for a day or two more, but after that she may become difficult. It is not that she loved Taudrille so much, as that she regards him as a brave French *agent* who has met his death at the hands of Nazis. She thinks the country round here is thick with them."

O'Mara said: "Maybe she's right."

Tanga de Sarieux appeared at the open french windows of the dining-room. She beckoned to O'Mara. He went across the lawn towards her.

She said: "Mr. Quayle has been on the telephone—just now. I told him that you were talking to Ernest Guelvada, and he said that I was not to disturb you. But he would like you to telephone him some time to-night."

O'Mara asked: "What else?"

"He gave me the address of his new headquarters," she said. "I was to tell you, and he would like Ernest Guelvada to know—in case of accidents. The address is Melissande House, St. John's Wood, London."

O'Mara asked. "Was that all?"

She shook her head. "Eleanor Frayne has been shot dead," she said. "Mr. Quayle said that it was obvious that they had followed her to her home from the old headquarters in Pall Mall; that they kept her under observation, hoping she would lead them to the new place. Apparently she was going on duty late at night. She thought she was being followed. She walked on until she saw a policeman and then she went towards him. The man following her shot and killed her. He tried to shoot the officer but was disarmed."

O'Mara asked: "Did they find anything on him?"

"Yes," she replied. "They found a coded note. It said that he must act; everything depended on him. Mr. Quayle considers that this man was probably the last agent in England; that they were relying on him; that he took a last desperate chance to reach Mr. Quayle."

O'Mara said: "I think that's right. They haven't got many people. He was probably the last. We must see that no more get over there."

"Poor little Frayne," she said. "Such a pretty girl." She asked: "Will you have dinner now?"

O'Mara nodded.

"Guelvada's going into Saint Lys," he said. "He's going to see the play again and have supper with his new girl friend."

He followed her into the dining-room.

He spoke little during dinner. But when Yvette had served coffee and departed, he said: "You'd better keep inside the house after dark. Don't walk about the grounds. It is possible that someone may take a shot at you. I don't want you killed unnecessarily."

She smiled at him. She said: "I will be careful, I do not want to be killed unnecessarily either. You think that the man who tried to shoot you last night . . .?"

"No," said O'Mara. "He's dead. Guelvada fixed him with that little knife of his. That wasn't so good."

"Not so good?" she queried. "You do not like that?"

"No," said O'Mara. "I believe the man was a *Maquisard*."

She raised her eyebrows. "A *Maquisard!* But how . . .?"

"Exactly," said O'Mara. "But how . . .?" The note of ill temper disappeared from his voice. He grinned across the table at her. "It would be damned hard luck, after six years of war, to be shot by a *Maquisard*. So stay inside."

"Very well," she said. "Let me give you some more coffee." She refilled his cup. "You are not happy, O'Mara . . ."

O'Mara got up. He began to walk about the room.

He said: "I'm damned unhappy. I can't get my teeth into anything. I've had bad luck from the start. I oughtn't to have killed Taudrille. I ought to have been in a position to wait and see what he would do. But I couldn't. I *had* to finish him or he'd have finished me. But it was a bad start. I'm like a man in a dark room trying to find a negro dressed in black. I don't know where the hell to start looking."

She said: "You've had bad luck, O'Mara. It will change."

He said: "I hope it changes in time." He got up; lit her cigarette and his cigar. He returned to his chair. He went on: "They've killed somebody they mistook for Quayle; they've killed the Frayne girl. Give 'em long enough and they'll get somebody over to England who *will* get Quayle. If they do get him it'll be as bad as losing an Army Corps. We need people like Quayle. We need them just as much in these days as we did in the worst days of the war. . . ."

She said softly: "*Something* will happen, O'Mara."

"I hope it will be the right thing," he said. "And I hope it will happen in good time. In any event, that doesn't help me now. I've got to *make* something happen. It was to *make* something happen that I've been drinking bad liquor; eating filth for food; existing like a dog at the *Garage Volanon* for ten months. To *make* something happen."

He laughed. She saw that his eyes were bright with anger.

"Well, something's happened. They've killed an inoffensive Pole, and Eleanor Frayne is no longer interested in interior decoration, and that's as far as we've got."

He got up. He said: "The most difficult thing in the world is to do nothing. Masterly inactivity. It doesn't suit me."

She said: "How can you talk about doing nothing? You're badly hurt and you never stop working and thinking. You have no need to reproach yourself. Has Guelvada discovered nothing? This girl Ernestine . . ."

"A stalemate," said O'Mara tersely. "The girl Ernestine . . . what do we *know* about her? She may be everything Guelvada thinks she is. She may be a decent French girl who was fooled by Taudrille. And she may not. How do we know? And how can we find out? By doing nothing and waiting. By seeing what happens. Maybe we'll find out soon enough, perhaps Guelvada, with all his quickness and cleverness, will be found at the bottom of a cliff. Then we'll know."

She said: "You can do nothing but wait. There is nothing you *can* do but wait."

"I can't afford to wait," said O'Mara. "*They're* not waiting."

"This is the time to relax, O'Mara," she said. "If you can. You are like an impatient tiger."

He got up from his chair. He looked at his wrist-watch. He said: "It's just after nine o'clock. In a few minutes Volanon will begin to lock up the garage. Then, if there are no customers in the café, he will go to the *Nouveau Café*. I'm going to get him before he leaves the garage."

"And then?" she asked.

"He's going to talk and like it," said O'Mara. "He must know something. He *has* to know something. However small or unimportant it may be, it may do *some* good."

She said quietly: "Perhaps you are right."

"Don't go outside the Villa," said O'Mara. "Keep Yvette here too. Don't take any chances. Jean Larue will be here at ten-thirty. He will come from Gouarec on his bicycle, by the Gourant Farm road. He won't go near Saint Brieuc. When he arrives, he will come in by the side gate on the kitchen-garden side, walk across the lawn in the shadow of the garden wall at the end, and knock at this window. When you let him in you'd better have the light turned out. I shall be back by then."

She nodded. "I understand," she said. "Good luck to you, O'Mara."

He said: "Thanks." He went out by the french windows.

He walked quickly to the garage; started up the Typhoon; drove out by the front drive. He took the Gourant Saint Brieuc road—a secondary road that was usually deserted at this time of night. He accelerated to fifty. After two miles he turned on to the dirt road that by-passed the fishing cottages and led towards the left fork of the estuary.

He was thinking about Volanon. Volanon might have been making his own enquiries. He *might* have done this. It was possible. But if not, then his meeting with O'Mara at Taudrille's cottage was more than a coincidence. And he might know something else. Two-thirds of the fishing population in Saint Brieuc had been in the Maquis. They had been more than a thorn in the side of the German troops during the war. They had been as consistent in their dealing with traitors and extreme collaborators since. Some of these men may have known something. If so, it would get to Volanon's ears. Volanon knew everything. He was a great talker and a good listener.

O'Mara parked the car in the shadow of a wall a hundred yards or so from the beginning of the estuary road. He walked down the road, keeping in the shadows, with a wary eye for a late straggler from the fishing boats. The road was deserted. The moon was good and the wide waters of the estuary lapped peacefully against the walls of the small harbour basin.

The road narrowed. Now O'Mara was only fifty yards from the *Café Volanon*. But there was no light in the window. It was shut. He passed the café. The doors of the *Garage Volanon* were locked, but above the garage, from Volanon's room, came a light.

O'Mara, stepping carefully, moved round to the side of the garage, pushed open the small wooden door in the side wall—a door which was seldom locked; went in. He closed the door behind him; stood in the darkness. He walked softly across the garage to Volanon's ramshackle office, switched on the dim light. The office was empty, the table covered with the usual litter of newspapers, catalogues, pens that did not write, unsharpened pencil stubs.

He came out of the office; mounted the stairs. He walked along the passage; looked into his own room, then into Volanon's— where the light was on. He went into the tiny kitchen at the end, and the storeroom, filled with old tyres and odd junk.

The place was deserted. But if the light was on in Volanon's room, he would be returning soon. He was too mean to waste electric current.

O'Mara went downstairs, out of the side door, began to walk along the arm of the estuary towards the sea.

He was angry. He was angry because he disliked to bring unknown quantities into a business which already presented too many unknown aspects. But he saw no other method. His instinct told him that something must be done quickly.

Now the road had narrowed to a footpath which bounded the water edge. The path sloped deeply towards the water a few feet beneath. Here and there were bushes, trees overhanging the water, iron-shod stakes that the Germans had used for mooring light craft.

O'Mara pushed his way through a clump of bushes; stood on the grass verge; looked across the still waters of the estuary. He thought that by the time he had returned to the garage Volanon might be back.

He turned; looked down; realised that he need not bother. The dead face of Volanon looked up at him from the shallow water. The eyes were open and the tight black beret, waterlogged, clung closely to the big head.

Volanon, thought O'Mara, had acquired a certain dignity with death. The eyes were open and staring, but even their stark expression and the attitude of the head, which sagged strangely to one side, could not mar an impression that was nobler than that which Volanon had worn during his life.

O'Mara sighed angrily. He pulled up his trousers legs, kicked a couple of footholds in the grassy bank with his heels, stepped down into the water. He put his hand into the neckband of Volanon's wet and dirty shirt; pulled the body round; stood in a foot of water, looking at the dead face.

The Breton had been stabbed in the neck. The wound was large and jagged—the work of an amateur with a knife. The throat was torn where the knife had been twisted and pulled out, but the original clean incision showed on one side.

O'Mara straightened up; looked about him. He began to splash his way along the edge of the estuary, keeping close into the bank. He moved along for a few yards; then stopped. He saw where Volanon had been killed.

The bank was gouged with muddy footmarks that had slithered and been able to obtain a foothold. Just above, a tree stood, and one branch overhung the estuary. Volanon had been pushed, or had slipped, into the water; possibly the push had appeared to be accidental. He had moved along to the tree, seized the branch, tried to climb up. Someone standing above him, on the bank, had allowed him nearly to reach the top, and then, when Volanon was engaged in trying to obtain a foothold, stabbed him in the throat. Volanon had fallen backwards to die in the water.

O'Mara reached up for the branch; pulled himself up the bank; examined the grass verge at the top. There was no sign of any struggle, only one or two indistinct footmarks on the dusty grass.

Something white caught his eye. He bent down and picked it up. It was a small paper envelope an inch square. Printed on it in French were the words *"Dr. Veniot's Headache Cachet."* O'Mara stood on the edge of the bank, the tiny envelope in his hands, his eyes searching the ground.

A few inches down the bank, towards the water, caught in the grass, was a silver pencil. He leaned down, picked it up. O'Mara thought that the headache cachet and the pencil might have fallen from the pockets of the killer as he had bent over the bank to finish off Volanon.

He took off his coat, rolled up his shirt sleeves, climbed down into the water. He stood away from the bank, the water nearly up to his knees. He put his right hand beneath the water, immediately under the place where the footmarks showed. He ran his hand over the sandy bottom of the estuary, picking up pieces of twigs, seaweed, stones; examining them, throwing them away. He continued searching.

His fingers touched something, closed on it, brought it to the surface. It was a small book, bound in black leather. O'Mara looked at it, put it in his pocket. He searched under the water for another five minutes; then climbed out, put on his coat, shook the water from his wet legs and shoes, began to walk back to the garage.

For the first time in his life a certain hopelessness began to possess O'Mara. The sensation was a new one. He did not like it. Nothing went right. Nothing worked. O'Mara, who had always been the producer of action, now found himself in the position of an onlooker whilst others acted. Each attempt to create a situation from which logical action might emerge was thwarted by a quicker step from the other side.

He went into the garage by the side door, bolted it behind him. He searched the lower floor carefully. The place was undisturbed. He went upstairs, looked into the upper rooms, turned off the light in Volanon's room. He came down the stairs in the darkness, went into the garage office, switched on the light.

He took the leather book from his pocket; opened it. In spite of the water he could read the words on the title page distinctly: *A pocket edition of The Works of William Shakespeare.*

O'Mara began to look through the book. The corner of one of the pages was turned down. The play was *Romeo and Juliet.* He examined the page carefully; then began to read, scanned through the close type, stopped. The words before him burned in his brain. . . . *"What's in a name? That which we call a rose by any other name would smell as sweet . . ."*

So Volanon's killer had been interested in the Works of Shakespeare, and the page was turned down at that quotation.

O'Mara remembered the Polish translation that he had read in Taudrille's cottage. Korsak's Polish translation, done in Vilna in 1840, the translation which, put into literal English, read: *"What's in a name? A rose, although its name be altered, will it not crimson for me with enchanting colour?"*

Not a very good translation; not as good as the original English of William Shakespeare, but nevertheless a translation of a sort.

The translation was in fact characteristic of its Polish translator. An artist in words, Korsak. It had sounded prettier to him to say that a rose "crimsoned with enchanting colour" rather than it "smelt as sweet." Perhaps he did not like the word "smell"; perhaps he was fond of the word "crimsoned"—a word beloved by poets.

O'Mara began to think about the word "crimson." For some mysterious reason the word stayed in his mind . . . *crimson* . . . *crimson.* . . . What was there about the word?

O'Mara sat in the dusty, paper-littered office, under the dim lamp, the book in his hand, looking straight in front of him. He fumbled in his pocket for a cigarette, lit it. If there was a connection between the Shakespeare of Taudrille—the Nazi who read only the *Life of Napoleon* and Korsak's Polish Edition of Shakespeare—and the English pocket edition of the killer of Volanon—what was it?

If there *was* a connection.

And there must be. The long arm of coincidence could not be as long as that!

O'Mara repeated to himself the original lines from Korsak— Korsak, who preferred to talk about "roses crimsoning for him with enchanting colour" instead of roses smelling as sweet:

"Co po imieniu? Roza choc naz wisko mieni
Czyliz sie, mniej powabnym kolorem rumieni?"

He said to himself: "By God!"

He began to grin. He drew his lips back over his teeth like a wolf.

He put the leather book in his pocket.

He reached out for the telephone; sat waiting, his eyes scanning the rubbish on the table in front of him, but not seeing it.

Yvette's voice came on the telephone.

O'Mara said: "Yvette, ask Madame to come to the telephone quickly. This is Monsieur O'Mara."

She said: "Yes."

He waited impatiently, his foot tapping the floor. Tanga came on the line.

He said: "I've had a bit of luck. We've got to move quickly."

She said: "I am glad."

O'Mara went on: "Is Larue there?"

"Yes. He was early. He was here ten minutes ago."

He asked: "What do you think of him?"

"I like him. He is a Breton. I think you will find he is very hard—what you call tough—*formidable.*"

"Why was he early?" asked O'Mara.

"He had some work to do," she said, "at Saint Lys. He is a photographer. He also does work for the police. It is rather amusing, but apparently he has been making photographs of the bodies of our friend Taudrille and the man Nago, whom it seems was discovered in a wood. So he had to be at Saint Lys. He came straight from there on his bicycle."

O'Mara said: "I wonder if my luck's going to hold. I wonder if he's got his camera with him."

She said: "Wait a minute. I will find out."

He waited. When she came back she said: "Yes, he has everything on the back of his bicycle."

O'Mara said: "Good. That's going to save a lot of time. I want you and Larue to come down here. I'm speaking from Volanon's garage. How can you get down?"

"Larue has his bicycle. Yvette has another. I can ride a bicycle. I do not like the process, but I can do it at a pinch."

O'Mara said: "This is a pinch. You'll ride the bicycle."

She laughed. She said: "Very well, M'sieu."

He went on: "Put on a coat and skirt; alter your appearance just a little—not too much. Alter your hair style; wear a blouse or something that is unlike what you usually wear. I want you to look different, but yet to be recognised as *you*. You understand?"

She said: "Perfectly."

"Come down by the Gourant Farm road," said O'Mara. "There is no one about here. Volanon's not here. I've left the car against a wall down at the end of the estuary road. You'd better leave the bicycles there. Tell Larue to bring his camera with him. Come here on foot. Keep out of sight. Try not to be seen. Come in by the side door to the garage."

She said: "Very well." She sighed. "Is there going to be a little excitement?"

O'Mara said: "Plenty."

"I am glad," she said. "I was getting a little bored."

O'Mara said: "I'm sorry to hear that. Perhaps your guests bore you."

She said: "Not at all. On the contrary—only the situation. In fact I was thinking—" She hesitated.

O'Mara asked: "What were you thinking?"

She said airily: "I was thinking that if the situation progressed a little, possibly my guests—as you call them—might be more amusing. *Au revoir*."

O'Mara hung up. He sat in the dusty office, smoking a cigarette, thinking of Rozanski, trying to visualise what he looked like.

It was ten-thirty. Guelvada, leaning against the wall opposite the stage door of the little theatre in Saint Lys, watched Ernestine as she tripped along the passage that led from back-stage to the stage-door entrance. He went to meet her.

He said: *"Man petit chou*, every time I see you, you look more delightful. You are a wonderful person. You are full of energy; you radiate happiness. You enchant me."

She smiled. She said: "I think it is funny your name should be Ernest and mine Ernestine." She spoke softly, with the trained diction of an actress. He thought she had a charming voice.

They began to walk towards her house. Outside the theatre, a little crowd of people stood on the pavement before dispersing to their homes.

She said: "They have a great deal to talk about. Everybody is now talking about the discovery of Nago's body. Everybody is talking about my poor Jules. They are connecting the two things."

Guelvada said: "Yes? Why should they do that? There is no necessity for the two things to be connected."

She looked at him. She said: "Don't *you* believe that the same man has killed both of them?"

Guelvada said: "It may well be, but one is never certain. That is a thing which I learnt years ago when I began the work I am doing now. One must never be certain until one is quite sure. It is so easy to jump to conclusions."

She said: "Ernest, I assure you that my instinct is right. The murderer is the same."

Guelvada asked: "Why do you think that?"

She said: "Obviously—the two suicide notes. The note found on Nago's body was apparently written in his own handwriting. The sergeant at the police, who is my friend, tells me that there was a notebook on him. The handwriting in the notebook and the suicide note was the same—or appeared to be the same. You understand that?"

Guelvada nodded.

"Very well," she went on. "Consider the fact that the suicide note found on Jules was also in *his* handwriting—or appeared to be in his handwriting."

Guelvada said: "Do you think that Taudrille did not write that note himself? Do you think that somebody may have forged his handwriting and also Nago's; or alternatively, do you think that somebody forced Taudrille to write that note?"

She shook her head. "No one could force Jules to do anything," she said. "He was a splendid man. I think someone imitated his handwriting. I think that the murderer knew Nago well. I think he knew their handwritings. I think that he was an expert with his pen, possibly a forger—someone who had been used to forging documents—a spy. You know how well these Nazis are trained."

Guelvada said: "You really think this is the work of a Nazi spy? You think there are lots of them about?"

She put her arm through his. She said: "Of course. You ought to know that, especially in this part of the country. Think of the hundreds and thousands of men who were employed by that filthy Hitler in his Gestapo; think of the hundreds and thousands of men who were used by the vile Himmler—men whose whole lives had been devoted to every sort of sordid business. Don't you realise that there must be thousands of these men who are still free; thousands of them trying to believe that the *régime* under which they lived and worked is still possible; deluding themselves into the belief that they can create it? You know what the Germans say—'Once a Nazi always a Nazi.'"

Guelvada nodded his head. He said: "That is true."

"What is more reasonable," she went on, "than that they should come here—here in the country? These desolate places like Saint Brieuc, and the country round about, were made for them. They can hide. They can plot. My poor Jules was working here. He knew they were here. You should know that."

Guelvada thought he was on delicate ground. He trod carefully. He said: "I would not say that Jules *knew* they were here. He had an idea that they were here. He was trying to find them."

She said: "I believe it is my duty to go to the police. I believe that I ought to tell them about Jules. I believe I ought to tell them that it was I who found his body; that I removed that suicide note. I ought to show it to them; to let them see that the two suicide notes are identical."

Guelvada pretended to consider the matter. They turned into the lane, hedged on each side, that led towards her small house.

He said: "Perhaps that will be a good thing for you to do. But not yet."

She said: "No?" She raised her eyebrows. "Tell me why, Ernest."

He said: "I will tell you. Perhaps I should not be talking about this, because my work, like that of my poor friend Taudrille, is secret, but I have an idea that I may be able to put my hand on the murderer. I do not want interference at this moment—from the police or anyone else. I want only two or three days. Then I think I shall strike. You must wait till then."

She said: "Very well, I will do that." She took out her key; opened the door. He followed her into the passageway; switched on the light.

She said: "I wonder why I do just what you tell me." She looked at him.

Guelvada thought that her eyes were soft. He said: "I'll tell you—or rather I won't tell you. I'd like to tell you—but—" He shrugged his shoulders. "If I did you wouldn't believe me."

She smiled. She said: "Tell me, Ernest; then I will tell you whether I believe you or not."

Guelvada arranged his voice so that it exuded sentimentality. His eyes became soft. He said: "The reason is simple. In your heart, my delightful Ernestine, there is a little affection for me—just a little. Unfortunately, you do not give that affection full play. You do not allow it to possess you because always you are remembering your dead lover." Guelvada looked very sorrowful. "I remember him too. He was my friend—my companion. We had lived and worked together. But it is not good for me." He sighed. "I would like you not to remember him too much," he went on. "I would prefer to believe that you wanted to think of me."

She said: "It is funny you should say that. I do think of you. I found myself thinking about you last night." She cast down her eyes. "I found myself thinking about you too much."

Guelvada took his cue. He reached out for her. She put her arms round his neck. They stood in the shabby little hallway embracing each other, their mouths pressed together.

Guelvada thought she kissed very well. He thought there were moments when his work had its compensations.

*

The clock in the church tower on the far side of the estuary struck eleven. The sound came over the quiet waters, accentuating the stillness of the night. O'Mara, sitting in Volanon's office, an unlit cigarette in his mouth, heard the soft tap-tap on the side door of the garage. He got up, stretched, crossed the garage floor, opened the door.

Tanga and Jean Larue came into the garage. O'Mara closed and bolted the door behind them.

She said: "This is Monsieur Jean Marie Larue."

O'Mara held out his hand. "I'm glad to meet you," he said. "Monsieur Guy Varin of the Second Bureau said that I could count on your assistance."

Larue said: "I am at your disposal. Monsieur Varin has conveyed a message to me about you. I am instructed to do everything I can. It will give me great pleasure to do anything against those pigs."

O'Mara liked the look of Larue. He was short, dark, intelligent. His eyes were quick. There was a scar of a knife slash across his face.

O'Mara said: "Come with me." He led the way across the dark floor to the office in the corner. He sat down on the chair, lit the cigarette in his mouth. He looked at Tanga.

She wore a dark coat and skirt, a shirt blouse with a small bow at the neck. She had dressed her hair up to the top of her head in soft curls. She had made up her eyelids with a middle-blue colour, extended the eyes, narrowed them by a suggestion of colour at the ends. The shape of her mouth had been altered slightly by the clever use of a different shade of lipstick. The dark pencil-lining under her eyes, carefully shaded down, had sunk them a little; gave her the appearance of being a little older and a great deal more wicked. She had lined out her nostrils with a lake-coloured grease-paint which enlarged them, altered slightly the shape of her nose.

She said: "Well . . . will I do?"

"It's good," said O'Mara. "You look like you—yet you are different."

He got up. He gave cigarettes to Tanga and Larue, lit them. He brought in two stools from the garage. They sat down.

O'Mara said: "Larue . . . the man Taudrille who was found at the foot of the cliff at the church was a Nazi agent. There was an enlargement of a micro-photograph on him. The police will have it. Can you get it?"

Larue grinned. "I have it," he said. "You do not know, of course, that I am the police photographer. During the Occupation I managed to photograph most of the S.S. and Army chiefs in this area. Those pictures helped to bring them to death or trial. I photographed Taudrille on the slab at the police morgue in Saint Lys. I also photographed the body of the man called Nago."

O'Mara said: "All this is lucky. Do you think you could fake a photograph? Could you take a picture of me, transpose the head of Taudrille from the photograph you have so that it would look all right?"

"Not from the picture that was found on Taudrille," said Larue. "But from another picture I took of him. I took three pictures of the body in the morgue. A full-length and two pictures of the face. The last one could be used for the fake picture. Half of his face was good and the other half smashed in. I can retake a photograph of the good side picture which I have, and put it on your body. That is easy."

"All right," said O'Mara. "Do that. We'll give you the picture I want in a minute. Then, when you've taken it, transpose the head of Taudrille for my head. We were more or less alike in build, and if you only take the upper half of the body it will do. Then reduce that picture on to a micro-film. Then photograph a typewritten description which I shall give you in a minute and reproduce it in small detail on the back of the micro-photograph. You understand?"

"Perfectly," said Larue. "You want the same sort of micro-picture that we in the *Maquis* used to carry. Something that is small enough to be easily hidden and just big enough to be recognised by the naked eye. All that is easy."

"Good," said O'Mara. "Can you do all that and let me have the micro-photograph complete with the typescript on the back by to-morrow afternoon?"

"Yes," said Larue. "If I work all night to-night. And I shall be glad to do that."

"Excellent," said O'Mara. "Then I rely on the micro-photograph complete being delivered at the *Villa Cote d'Azur* by three o'clock to-morrow afternoon. Remember it is a matter of life and death."

Larue nodded. "It shall be done," he said. "You have the word of Jean Marie Larue."

O'Mara lit a fresh cigarette. He thought that it *was* a matter of life and death. Of life *or* death. He wondered whose life and whose death.

He said: "Get your camera, Larue. Let's go to work."

Larue picked up his camera; began to prepare it. O'Mara arranged the dilapidated furniture in the office. He arranged the chair with the back close to the table set against the whitewashed wall. One or two small poster advertisements for tyres, and the picture of a car, on the wall, added a touch of colour. He went upstairs, collected from the kitchen two tumblers and a few empty wine bottles. He brought them down, with a cigarette ash-tray; arranged them on the table.

He smoked his cigarette rapidly; put the half-smoked end, still alight, with a tendril of smoke curling upwards, in the ash-tray. He collected odd cigarette stubs from the floor; put them in the ash-tray. He laid one wine bottle on its side as if it had been knocked over.

He said to Tanga: "Come here." He sat down in the chair, looking at her closely as she stood before him. He put his hands on her waist."

He said: "You look delightful."

She looked down at him. The tone in which the words had been spoken belied them. O'Mara's face was grim.

She said with a little smile: "Thank you, M'sieu. . . ."

"But," said O'Mara, "you are not wanton enough. We shall have to do something about that. Give me your lipstick."

She took a small compact and lipstick case from the pocket of her jacket. O'Mara took the lipstick, accentuated the cupid's bow of her mouth. He stood back from her; looked at his handiwork.

He said: "That's better." He moved towards her, disarranged her hair a little. He undid her coat; removed the bow from the neck of her shirt blouse; undid the top two buttons.

She said: "I must be a very bad woman, O'Mara."

He grinned at her. He said: "You'd be surprised. Now sit down, both of you. Listen to me."

They sat down on the stools which O'Mara had moved to the other end of the office. He stood facing them.

He said: "The story is this. I am Taudrille. With the upper part of my body only showing and Taudrille's head transposed, that will be good enough. It is known to a woman—Tanga de Sarieux—that I am a German agent, so she tries to do something about it. What she is trying to do is to get a photograph taken of Taudrille with herself, so that both he and she may be identified by it. That is the picture we have to take. We shall take the picture in this office, because this wall showing these tyre advertisements and the picture of a car will identify it. *Somebody* has been in this office—somebody whose eyes are very keen will have noted those advertisements on the wall. They will recognise the scene, and by recognising the scene *they will know the photograph is a fake*. They will realise it was taken for their own especial benefit. You understand?"

Tanga nodded.

Larue said: "Perfectly. The photograph is to be very good. Everything about it is perfect except the fact that it was taken in this office; except the fact that someone can recognise the scene and therefore will know that the photograph is a fake."

"Right," said O'Mara. "Are you ready, Larue?"

Larue got up; took up his camera. The bulb flash was fixed. He said: "The light is very bad here. I must use a flash. I shall count one two three four five. I shall photograph on five. Will you get ready?"

O'Mara said: "Tanga, come here. Look at the table. See the half-smoked cigarette still smoking, the cigarette stubs. You and

I have been in this office. I am Taudrille and you have been trying to make me talk. We have been drinking a little, you and I. You realise that the time has come to strike. You are leaning against the table, and I am sitting in the chair. You move from the table. You sit yourself on my knee. You put your arms round my neck. You kiss me in such a way that you are hiding a little of my face but not enough for me not to be recognised as Taudrille." He grinned at her. "And make it look real," he said.

Tanga sighed. Her mouth quivered a little. She said: "The things I do for France."

She sat on O'Mara's knee. She put her arms round his neck. Larue focused his camera. He began to count one . . . two . . . three."

O'Mara said: "Give, Tanga. . . ."

Their lips met as Larue set off the flash.

O'Mara asked: "All right, Larue?"

"Pretty good, I think," he said. "But we'll do it again."

O'Mara said: "Once more, Tanga." He looked at her mischievously He said: "I'm sorry about this."

She raised her eyebrows. She said: "Really . . . why?"

The second photograph was taken. Then O'Mara said: "Larue, get back to Gouarec. Try not to be seen. That should not be difficult. There's no one much about these parts at night. You'd better go now. Don't forget, I've got to have that picture by three o'clock to-morrow afternoon."

Larue said: "I have given my word. But what about the typescript on the back?"

O'Mara said: "I'm going to do that now." He went to the cupboard at the far end of the office; brought out a dilapidated typewriter. He searched in the untidy table drawer for a piece of paper; put it into the machine. He began to type:

"Photograph of Jules Francois Taudrille. A Nazi Agent. Operated in the Gouarec-Saint Lys-Saint Brieuc districts. Taken with an operative of a British Special Service Section to be identified with real name and description by Second Bureau if possible. Please act quickly."

He took out the sheet of notepaper, read it through, handed it to Larue.

Larue said: "I will not put this on the back of the micro-photograph. That would not be good. I will do a second micro-photograph attached to the first film by a perforation. That is what we usually do. It will look very good."

"All right," said O'Mara. "You've done good work, Larue. Thank you."

They shook hands.

Larue said: "Whatever you're doing, M'sieu . . . good luck. Our good wishes go with you."

He put his camera in its case; slung it over his shoulder.

O'Mara said: "Just a minute. Last night a too enthusiastic member of the *Maquis* took a shot at me as I was going into the Villa. He thought I was a Nazi. He had been told that. It is very unfortunate, but he was killed by my associate."

Larue shrugged his shoulders. "That would be young Dupont—Gaston Dupont. It was the same in the war. Always he wanted to kill somebody too quickly. He never thought. As you say, it is unfortunate, but we shall understand. After all, he thought he died for France. *Au'voir!* " He went out.

O'Mara lit a cigarette. He stood leaning against the wall, his hands in his pockets.

She said: "O'Mara . . . I think you are a little happier."

He smiled at her. He said: "Our business has its compensations—even if they are whittled down by circumstances. I would prefer to kiss you not in front of a camera."

She said: "I have no doubt."

"You'd better go now," said O'Mara. "Get your bicycle and ride back to the Villa. You'd better go in by the front entrance."

She asked: "And you?"

He said: "I shall be coming back soon."

"I think it is extremely hard," said Tanga, "that I should have to pedal a bicycle uphill whilst you ride luxuriously in my Typhoon."

O'Mara said tersely: "On your way."

She went out. She thought that whatever was in O'Mara's mind was a very grim thing.

*

It was one o'clock. O'Mara paced up and down his bedroom, his hands in his dressing-gown pockets, an unlit cigar in his mouth. The large, silver coffee-pot on the dressing-table was empty.

He thought that life was often hard; that when it was hard it was *damned hard*. A thing happened and you had to do something about it and you couldn't consider things or people. That was how it was. He remembered his encounter with Morosc and Nago. He remembered the cigarette lighter held between his fingers. . . .

The things in his mind were not pleasant. But it had to be like that, no matter what happened. It had to be played that way.

Tanga tapped on the door. She called softly: "He's on the line. Will you take it from my room or downstairs? Is there anything else for me to do?"

O'Mara said brusquely: "No. Go to bed." He went out into the corridor; down the stairs. As she went into her room he heard her murmur: "Such a pig . . ."

He picked up the receiver. Quayle's voice came over the line. O'Mara said: "Listen, Peter. . . . This is going to be tough."

"Yes . . .?" said Quayle.

O'Mara went on: "I've got a line at last. A definite line. And there's only one thing to be done about it. There's only one way I can find out. I've got to bait the hook."

"I see," said Quayle. "What's the bait and how important is the fish?"

"The fish is very important," said O'Mara. "The bait has got to be good. I don't like it, but there's no other way. I've got to give 'em Guelvada and the woman. . . ." His voice was unhappy.

Quayle said: "If you've got to you've got to. We're all in the same boat. They both knew what the job might be like when they went into it. If you *must* do it . . ."

"Damn you," said O'Mara harshly. "D'you think I *want* to?"

"Take it easy, Shaun," said Quayle. His voice was calm. "You'll do what you think is right. The consequences must take care of themselves. It's a chance we all take. Do you want anything?"

"Plenty," said O'Mara. "Listen carefully, Peter. This is the last chance I shall get to talk to you. You've got to get a plane over to

France between now and to-morrow morning—to Paris. A four-seater cabin plane. With an intelligent pilot. Have you got that?"

"I've got it," said Quayle. "And then?"

"The pilot has to go to the Embassy in Paris. He must get two Military Movement Orders signed. They've got to be blank orders with no names filled in. That can be done later. Also he must pick up a couple of blank passports visaed for Great Britain, and stamped, so that anyone can fill in the descriptions and photographs. Understood?"

"Understood," said Quayle. "Go on."

"You've got to give the pilot a sealed letter when he leaves for Paris," said O'Mara. "You must write a personal note to me. You must tell me that the arrest of the man who shot Frayne has finished their operatives in England. That everything is O.K. You tell me to come back and bring my colleague with me. You want us at once. Have you got that?"

"I've got it," said Quayle.

"Right," said O'Mara. "Then the pilot goes to Paris; gets the Movement Orders and the blank visaed and signed passports from the Embassy in Paris. He can hang around for an hour or two and then he must take the plane up to Gouarec airstrip. The airstrip is just north of the town—two miles north."

Quayle said: "I know the place. We used it with the first S.A.S. during the war. It's quite a good strip."

"All right," said O'Mara. "The pilot lands there. He must land there not later than six o'clock to-morrow evening—with the documents I've mentioned. Needless to say he *must* be intelligent."

Quayle said: "Don't worry. He'll be very intelligent. I'll use Johnny Sager."

"Good," said O'Mara. "There's only one thing more. There are a couple of officials at the airstrip. Let somebody big give them the tip-off not to be too nosey about anything that happens. Let somebody tell 'em to mind their own business."

Quayle said: "The Gouarec airstrip isn't used for anything. The officials are only caretakers in fact. They won't interfere in any way. I'll fix that. Is that all?"

O'Mara said: "That's the lot. Well . . . so long, Peter."

Quayle said: "Just a minute, Shaun. About Guelvada and Tanga. If it's like you say it is, if you've got to use them for bait, don't tell them too much. It's always easier for people if they don't know."

O'Mara said grimly: "I don't intend to. Anyway, it isn't kind to tell people that. . . ."

Quayle said: "I know. I've done it myself. Quite a lot. It isn't nice."

There was a silence. Then O'Mara said: "Good night."

"Good night," said Quayle. "Good luck."

O'Mara hung up the receiver. He went up to his room. He sat on the bed and looked at the wall in front of him.

He thought that it was damned hard luck that he had ever begun to work for Quayle. He began to curse. He cursed everything and everybody.

It made no difference. Eventually he stopped. He sat, chewing the unlit cigar, looking at the wall.

The bright afternoon sun came through the french windows; marked the dining-room with gold and black shadows. Tanga de Sarieux was arranging flowers when O'Mara passed through the room. He had reached the french windows when she spoke.

She said: "Good morning, O'Mara . . . or should I say good afternoon? I think you did not sleep very well last night."

"No," said O'Mara. He stood blinking in the sunlight.

She went on: "Once in England I saw a play called *The Man with a Load of Mischief.* You remind me of that title. You look as if you have something very heavy on your shoulders—something that makes you unhappy."

O'Mara said: "Yes?" He began to say something; stopped. Then he went on: "If Larue comes, send him to me. I shall be walking about the garden."

She said: "Very well." She watched him as he walked across the lawn.

O'Mara walked up and down the gravel pathway that divided the far side of the lawn from the coppice. As far as he could see, after eight hours' thought, the plan was watertight—as watertight as any plan could be. Of course there was always the human element. His mind jerked away from that. He did not want to consider the human element.

He walked up and down the path like a restless animal. He was surprised at himself. He was surprised that O'Mara—the man who for years had been walking about the world with his life in his hands, and not only his own life but the lives of other people; who, when occasion demanded it, spent those lives as he would have spent his own, without so much as a second thought—now found himself in a quandary over a question that had but one answer. The job had got to be done.

He stopped; lit a cigarette. Jean Larue came across the lawn from the dining-room. He held a little leather document case in his hand. He was smiling.

He said: "But everything is perfect, M'sieu O'Mara. You are going to be pleased with my work. Let me show you."

They walked down one of the little paths into the shade of the trees. Larue opened the case; brought out an envelope. From the envelope he produced a small micro-photograph—one and a quarter inches square—joined to another film of the same size by a perforation.

He said: "Hold it to the light. It's a perfect picture. Then, if you want to, look at it through this glass."

O'Mara held the film up to the light. He said: "It's damned good work, Larue."

The picture was perfect. O'Mara could clearly discern the dusty office; could see the posters on the wall; could recognise the detail. The picture of himself with the woman in his arms, their mouths pressed together, was good in every detail, except that it was not his head. Obviously it was the face of Taudrille. He took the magnifying glass from Larue's hand; examined the micro-photograph through it.

He said: "You are a very good photographer, Larue. It's marvellous work. Give me an envelope."

He put the film in the envelope, the envelope in the breast pocket of his jacket.

He said: "Here is a good place to sit down. I want to talk to you. Before I begin, I want to tell you this. You wouldn't have been put in touch with me unless you were a good man. You are a good Frenchman—a patriot—of the *Maquis*. Remember what I am asking you to do is for France. Also remember that it is possible that the lives of good friends of France will depend on how carefully you carry out my instructions."

Larue said: "M'sieu O'Mara, you know my record. My son died fighting against the Germans. I have been against them right through the war years. People know what I have done in Brittany. I shall not fail you."

"I believe that," said O'Mara. They sat down on the green bank beneath a tree. O'Mara went on: "Listen to me, Larue. This is what you have to do. . . ."

It was seven o'clock when O'Mara arrived back at the Villa. He drove in by the front gate; put the car into the garage. He walked across the lawn, through the little door, along the passageway into Tanga's sitting-room.

Tanga and Guelvada were drinking cocktails.

She said: "You have just arrived in time. Ernest has made the most supreme cocktail—something he learned in Lisbon. Would you like one?"

O'Mara said: "No, thanks. I'd like a whisky and soda."

She poured out the drink; brought it to him. She said prettily. "Why don't you cheer up? Nothing is as bad as that."

He said: "I don't know that I want to cheer up. In any event, I don't have to try to be cheerful. That's a process that is worse than not being cheerful." He drank the whisky at a gulp. He said: "Ernest, I want to talk to you."

She said quickly: "Would you like me to go away?"

O'Mara said: "No. If I'd wanted you to go away I'd have told you." She shrugged her shoulders.

O'Mara led the way out on to the lawn.

Guelvada said: "Forgive me saying something which may seem a trifle impertinent. I have known you in some very tough situations, but I have never seen you perturbed. Is it as bad as that?"

O'Mara said: "I suppose so. I'm not particularly perturbed as you call it. I just don't like things, that's all."

Guelvada said: "I think I understand."

O'Mara said sharply: "What do you mean 'you think you understand?'"

Guelvada smiled. It was one of his most benign smiles. He said: "I have never known you to be perturbed for yourself. If you are perturbed, it is probably because of somebody else." He stood smiling at O'Mara. He looked quite happy.

O'Mara said: "Perhaps I am and perhaps I'm not. Does it matter?"

"No," said Guelvada. "It doesn't matter."

They began to walk along the path. When they were in the shadow of the trees, O'Mara produced the envelope from his pocket. He took out the micro-photograph, crumpled the envelope, threw it away. He handed the photograph to Guelvada.

He said: "Look at that."

Guelvada examined the picture. He said: "By God . . . this is marvellous. Who did it—Larue?"

O'Mara nodded. "It's nice work," he said. "I hope it succeeds."

Guelvada said: "What am I to do?"

"I'll tell you," said O'Mara. "To-night you're going to meet Ernestine. You will have in the inside pocket of your jacket an unsealed envelope with some documents in it. I will give you that in a minute. That envelope, with the top open, will be in the inside pocket of your jacket. Do you understand?"

"Why not?" said Guelvada. "That is very simple."

"All right," said O'Mara. "Now tell me about the geography of Ernestine's house. You ought to know it by now."

Guelvada smiled. "I know it well enough," he said. "You go in by the front door. It is a small house. When you close the door and stand with your back to it, you are looking down a passage which runs from the front to the back of the house—the usual thing. The door at the other end of the passage leads to the kitchen. There are two rooms on the right of the passage as you stand there at the door. The first one is the sitting-room. The door at the end of the passage before you walk into the kitchen is a bathroom. There is one door on the left-hand side of the passage. It leads to a bedroom. Farther along, and before you come to the kitchen, is a door which gives access to a little flight of steps leading to a loft—an odd sort of place which is used, I believe, to store boxes and things."

O'Mara said: "I see. And when you arrive at the house with Ernestine after the theatre, you go into the sitting-room?"

"That's right," said Guelvada. "We go into the sitting-room. Then, usually, she goes to the bedroom and takes off her things. While she is doing that"—he smiled—"being a domesticated person, I light the spirit lamp under the coffee percolator. Usually she comes back in two or three minutes."

"Very well," said O'Mara. "Remember this carefully. When you arrive at her house with her to-night, one button of your jacket will be nearly off. The thread will be frayed. As you get into the house you will pull the button right off; let it fall on the floor. You will give an exclamation of annoyance, stoop and pick up the button. You are a very neat person," O'Mara went on, "and you do not like a jacket without a button. You tell her about this. She will offer, I imagine, to sew it on for you."

"But of course," said Guelvada. "If she doesn't, I'll ask her to."

"It will make things easier," said O'Mara, "if on your way to the house you manage to slip and fall—get your hands dirty. When you have discovered that the button is missing, and when she offers to sew it on, or, alternatively, you ask her to sew it on, you will take off your coat and hand it to her—first to have the button sewn on, and secondly because you want to go to the bathroom to wash your hands. As you give her the coat you will arrange that this micro-photograph falls on the floor, but you will not notice it. You will go straight to the bathroom; wash your hands. You can take quite a time about that."

Guelvada said: "You mean I am to give her ample opportunity to examine the picture.?"

O'Mara nodded. "That's right," he said.

Guelvada said: "And the envelope with the documents."

"You will leave those in your inside jacket pocket when you hand it to her."

Guelvada said: "I see. If she wants to look at them while I am in the bathroom that's all right."

O'Mara said: "*If* she wants to look at them that's all right."

Guelvada thought for a moment; then he said: "And if not? Supposing I return from the bathroom, find her busily engaged in sewing on the button; supposing she has found the micro-photograph and hands it back to me saying nothing, showing that she has not looked at it, what do I do then?"

O'Mara said: "She'll have looked at it. She's a woman. Women are always curious. But just in case she's the exception that proves the rule, if she hands it back to you, ask her if she has looked at it. If she says no, tell her to look at it."

Guelvada asked: "You think that will happen?"

O'Mara said: "No, I don't. I think she'll look at the micro-photograph."

"And then?" Guelvada queried.

O'Mara shrugged his shoulders. "I don't know," he said. He looked at Guelvada. "Work it out for yourself, Ernest," he said. "Here is a woman who was in love with Taudrille. She tells us that she believes he was a good Frenchman. She loves him because he worked for France. She sees the photograph. She sees the man she loved in the arms of another woman. She recognises where the picture was taken."

Guelvada said: "Where was it taken? May I know?"

"In the office in Volanon's garage," said O'Mara.

Guelvada said: "But how should she know that scene? Has she been to the office?"

O'Mara smiled. "That's what I want to find out," he said. "If she looks at that micro-photograph; if she recognises the scene, which I think she will do, she'll have to do something about it."

"I see," said Guelvada. "So you think . . ."

"Never mind what I think," O'Mara, interrupted. His voice was almost harsh. "What I think and what you think doesn't matter. We've got to *know*. This way we'll find out."

Guelvada shrugged his shoulders. He said: "Of course. This is the way to find out." His voice lightened. He went on: "So I have returned from the bathroom, and for the sake of argument Ernestine has picked up the micro-photograph, has looked at it, has recognised her late lover in the arms of Madame la Comtesse.

Also she has recognised where the photograph was taken. She knows that the picture was taken in Volanon's garage. What does she do then?"

O'Mara said: "I don't know. That's another thing I want to find out."

There was a little pause. Guelvada said: "I've been many things in my life. I don't think I have ever been a guinea-pig before." He smiled whimsically. "So I am to be a guinea-pig—the unfortunate animal on which they try scientific experiments to find out things."

O'Mara said: "If you want to have it that way, that's how it is. You are a guinea-pig, Ernest."

Guelvada nodded his head. "I understand perfectly," he said. "Is there anything else?"

O'Mara said: "Yes. You had better go and pack your bag. You'd better go. Take the hired car, go back to Saint Lys, return the car to the place you hired it from. Go to the theatre. See your girl friend perform once more. Wait for her afterwards and take her home. On your way to her house suggest by your conversation that you may be leaving the district soon, but you hope not to be away for long; that you want to see her again. Make that sound good."

Guelvada said: "I'll make it sound very good. Is that all?"

"That's all," said O'Mara.

Guelvada took a small leather case from his pocket. He put the micro-photograph in the case. O'Mara handed him a stout envelope, opened at one end.

He said: "Put it in your pocket just like that."

Guelvada took the envelope; put it away. He said: "Well, I'll be on my way. I'll pack my bag, leave it in my bedroom. Then I'll get off."

O'Mara said: "So long, Ernie."

"So long," said Guelvada. He smiled at O'Mara. He said: "I shall not fail."

O'Mara watched him as he walked along the path, across the lawn.

O'Mara drank his coffee in silence. He put down his cup; looked at Tanga. He thought that she looked more lovely than ever in the soft light of the pink-shaded candles on the oak table. She wore a long dinner frock of daffodil-coloured chiffon. The full sleeves were caught in at the wrists with a narrow velvet ribbon, of the same colour as the amethyst sash which was tied in a bow in front, its long ends falling to her feet. Round her neck she wore a necklace of amethysts set in gold.

She said: "Do you realise you have said nothing during dinner? It is possible for one to think too much."

"I don't think so," said O'Mara. "Can I have some more coffee?" He went on: "That's a lovely frock, but I think you'd better change it after dinner."

She said: "Yes? But of course, if you say so. What am I to wear?"

"It doesn't matter very much," said O'Mara. "A coat and skirt. Anything like that."

She asked: "Why do I have to change? Am I not to know even that?"

O'Mara's voice was almost impatient. He said: "I'd like to remember the picture of you in that frock as you are now. Maybe I'm getting sentimental in my old age." He grinned at her. "But I'd like to think that that picture was unspoiled."

She said: "A most charming speech. Thank you, M'sieu . . . I will change into a coat and skirt immediately after dinner."

"You don't have to do it immediately after dinner," said O'Mara. "When I'm gone will do."

She raised her eyebrows. "So you are going, O'Mara?"

He got up from the table; brought her the cigarette box. He lit her cigarette.

He said: "Yes, I'm going. I've got to leave here to-night. I must be in Paris to-morrow morning." He was thinking to himself: I wonder if Quayle was right; whether it was better not to let people know what was in front of them; whether it affected their mentality—their courage. He looked at her. He thought nothing could affect the mentality or courage of Madame la Comtesse de Sarieux. He thought that, not because he *wanted* to think it, but because he believed it. He went back to his seat; lit his cigarette.

He said: "Tanga, I expect you're curious. I expect you think that I might have told you something about what's going on. I haven't told anybody for two reasons. The first—I didn't know. The second, I'm rather inclined to be like you—a good soldier—and obey orders. You know Quayle's technique. When an *agent* is walking into a very tough situation, unless it is absolutely necessary, he prefers that the operative should not know exactly what is in front of him—or her."

She drew on her cigarette, her elbow resting on the table, her long fingers drooping gracefully. She looked at him thoughtfully.

She said: "I know that sometimes it is a good thing. I said *sometimes*. It depends on the *agent*." She went on: "When Quayle sent you to Paris; when you started to drink in Paris; got into all that trouble when you were arrested, put into prison, released. When you worked your way across the country until you arrived here in Saint Brieuc; when you got that job at the *Garage Volanon*; wore those filthy clothes; ate that bad food; drank yourself into a stupor—you knew what might happen to you, didn't you, O'Mara? You knew that one day Morosc and Nago—or somebody else—would arrive. You knew what they would try to do to you. It did not affect your mentality. Am I not right?"

O'Mara looked at her. He said, with a touch of the old bravura: "I am O'Mara. I can do anything."

She said: "Precisely. Might I not suggest, with all humility, that I am de Sarieux?" She raised her head proudly. "I too can do anything."

O'Mara said: "That's as maybe, but you're still a woman."

She laughed. "Now you are becoming positively old-fashioned. And I like it better when you smile."

O'Mara said: "There's nothing much to smile about."

He got up; began to walk about the room.

She said: "I'm sorry I did not have the chance to say *au revoir* to Ernest Guelvada. I like him very much. Shall I see him again?"

O'Mara stopped walking. He stood with his elbow on the mantelpiece at the end of the room looking at her seriously.

He said: "I hope you'll see him again, Tanga. I too am very fond of Ernest." There was a silence; then he said: "Two nights ago I went to a cottage which Taudrille had used. It is about nine miles from the Saint Lys-Gouarec switch. I expect you know the road. I was in there looking around. I thought I might find something. I found nothing except two books in a bookcase. One was a translation into Polish by a man called Korsak of Vilna of Shakespeare's Plays done in 1840. I looked through the book. I know the Polish language very well. I was intrigued—not only intrigued—by what I considered to be a bad translation."

She said: "Yes? How interesting. What was it?"

O'Mara went on: "It was a translation of the lines from *Romeo and Juliet*. . . . 'What's in a name? That which we call a rose. . . by any other name would smell as sweet.'*

"Korsak had done the translation so that the lines read:

"'What's in a name? That which we call a rose
By any other name would crimson for me as enchantingly . . .'"

She said: "I think that is a delightful translation. Essentially Polish, and romantic, is it not?"

He nodded: "That's what I thought. After I had seen this book I was about to leave when I was surprised by Volanon." He laughed. "Papa Volanon with a pistol. He was going to kill me. Someone had told him that I was a Nazi."

She raised her eyebrows: "I wonder who that could have been."

"I wondered too," said O'Mara. "I had ideas—vague ideas—but I wasn't certain. I wondered how it was that Volanon knew that I should be at Taudrille's cottage at that time, or, alternatively, if he didn't know, what he was doing there. I made up my mind to ask him. But the first thing I had to do was to talk him out of squeezing the trigger of his automatic. I did. I talked him out of executing me. He went back on his bicycle to his garage. I told him I should be seeing him.

"That night, when I got back to the Villa, you remember someone took a pot shot at me as I came in through the gates. That was a young *Maquisard* by the name of Dupont, and it was obvious he had also been told I was a Nazi. You heard what I said to Larue last night. The man was young and enthusiastic. Unfortunately for him. At first I thought that Volanon and Dupont might have come to their conclusions about me because Desart—the man who helps the gardener here—had talked. I thought he might have talked in the *Nouveau Café*. But even if he told them that the Philippe Garenne of the *Garage Volanon* was staying at the Villa as a guest, there was no reason for them to suppose that I was a Nazi."

She said: "But of course not." She smiled at him mischievously. "There might have been another reason. I might have seen you at the garage when you were so delightfully drunk, and fallen in love with you. Why not?"

O'Mara laughed. "That, of course, would have been an excellent reason," he said. "What concerned me now was how Volanon had got the idea into his head. Then I came to a conclusion. Somebody had telephoned him at the garage and told him that the drunken Philippe Garenne who had been working for him for months was a Nazi. He had selected that method of hiding from French justice; that he had disappeared because the French *agent* Taudrille was on his track. That story is confirmed by the fact that Taudrille's body is found at the bottom of a cliff near the place where Garenne is known to have been —the yew-tree grove. So Volanon gets out his pistol and comes for Garenne."

She said: "That is reasonable."

O'Mara nodded. "Quite reasonable. Anyhow, I was able to talk Volanon out of killing me. Last night I went down to the garage to see him. A light was on in his room, but the garage was empty. I found him in the shallow waters of the estuary close in to the bank. He had been stabbed in the throat."

She said: "I see."

"Someone," continued O'Mara, "had been to see Volanon at a time when they knew the place would be deserted. That person had talked with him. Volanon had come down from his room and left the light on. He had come down when he saw this person outside the garage. They talked in the office; then they went for a walk together. They began to walk along the estuary bank, and after a little while this person, pretending that it was an accident, pushed Volanon into the estuary just a yard or two from a place where there is a tree overhanging the water—a tree that will help him to climb out. The person apologises, calls out to him that here is a tree which will help him out, and Volanon seizes one of the branches and begins to pull himself out.

"As he reaches the bank, the person stabs him in the throat, and in doing so drops a silver pencil, and a small book which fell into the water."

"Why should they go to all that trouble?" she asked. "It would have been easy for them to kill Volanon amongst the bushes on the bank?"

O'Mara said: "It would have been easy for a man—not for a woman. Remember that Volanon is big and quite strong."

She said: "So you think it was a woman?"

He nodded. He went on: "The important thing was the book. I found the book in the water. It was a small leather bound copy of Shakespeare's Plays, and a page was turned down at *Romeo and Juliet*—the page bearing the quotation . . . *'What's in a name? A rose by any other name would smell as sweet. . . .'*

"I wondered why Taudrille should have been so interested in that quotation which he had underlined and then erased the lines in his Polish translation, and why the person who killed Volanon should have had an English copy. Then suddenly I understood. It was one of those things which are so absurdly obvious that one doesn't notice."

O'Mara stopped speaking. The silence in the room was almost tense.

She said eventually: "What was it?"

"The man we are looking for," said O'Mara, "calls himself Rozanski. That is the name he has taken. The Polish for rose is Roza. But when a person is called Rose in the Polish language they are not called Roza. They are called Rozanski."

She said: "I see. And then?"

O'Mara said: "Remember the Korsak translation into Polish . . . *That which we call a rose by any other name would crimson as enchantingly. . . .'* 'Crimson' in the Polish quotation is *'rumieni.'* *'Rumieni'* translated into English means just 'crimson,' but a woman's name could not be 'crimson.' Just as *'roza'* applied to a man becomes Rozanski, so *'rumieni'* applied to a woman becomes 'Rumianska.'"

O'Mara added quietly: "The name of Guelvada's girl friend is Ernestine Rumianska."

She said softly: *"Mon Dieu . . .!"*

"Precisely," said O'Mara. "This was the code word. A rose by any other name would smell or crimson or be as sweet. Rozanski by any other name would be the same as Rumianska. In other words Rumianska is the representative of Rozanski. This was the international code by which, in any country, Rozanski's representative could be recognised."

She said: "And that is why you had that photograph taken last night at the garage?"

"Exactly," said O'Mara. "I believe the person who killed Volanon was Ernestine Rumianska. Guelvada took Taudrille's car back at her request and put it in the garage in the cottage. I believe she was on her way to get that car. She saw me going into the cottage, so she kept away. She found the telephone box that is on the Saint Lys road and telephoned to Volanon, who took his bicycle; got a lift on one of the fish-trucks probably as far as Saint Lys; finished the trip on his bicycle. He believed that I was the person who had killed Taudrille.

"But her plans did not come off. The next day O'Mara, or Garenne, is still alive. Now she wants to know why Volanon did not kill him. Now you see?"

She nodded. "I understand."

"So the next thing she does is to go to Volanon's garage to find out why. Volanon tells her why."

She said: "This is most interesting."

"It's going to be damned interesting," said O'Mara. "Guelvada's got that micro-photograph. To-night we have arranged a little play for he benefit of Mademoiselle Ernestine Duvallier—on the theatre bills—and Ernestine Rumianska in real life. Ernest is going to drop that photograph. Then he is going to her bathroom. She will pick up the photograph and examine it. She will see that it was taken in the office at Volanon's garage. She will recognise you. She will recognise Taudrille, and because that picture was taken in Volanon's office she will know it was a fake."

She said: "She will see that it was a trap for her?"

O'Mara nodded: "Then she's going to do something."

There was another silence. She put her cigarette in the ash-tray; took another; drew one of the pink-shaded candles towards her. She lit the cigarette. O'Mara saw the light play on her face.

She said: "I wonder what Ernestine will do then."

O'Mara thought: "To hell with Quayle. One must try to be fair." He said quietly: "My dear, I am going to tell you what I think she'll do. God knows, they're desperate enough now. When Guelvada comes back from the bathroom she'll be ripe for anything."

She said quickly: "She will kill Guelvada."

"She'll try to," said O'Mara. "She probably will. Then there is something else. She'll find something else on Guelvada—something which looks like a gift from the gods. She'll *have* to do something about it. There's only one thing she'll want to find out before she can get going—one thing she must find out. Remember that their last operative in England was caught following Eleanor Frayne, trying to find out where Quayle's new headquarters are. Well, Frayne was too good for him. He didn't find out. They cannot move until they know. If what I think is right, she'll have to find out. She'll come here."

She said: "I see . . ."

O'Mara left the mantelpiece. He walked over, stood beside her, looking down at her.

He said: "I'm damned sorry, Tanga. You know I'd like to do this myself. I can't. You've got to be the person who tells her. There's no other way."

She drew on her cigarette. She said: "It won't be the first hard situation I have been in, O'Mara. I've worked for Quayle for a long time, you know. And we all of us know what may be at the end of any road."

O'Mara said: "Right. The theatre finished at ten-thirty. If she's going to move it will be somewhere around midnight. You had better get Yvette out of here."

She said: "Yes, I'd thought of that. I will send her off within half an hour."

He said: "I must be going. I have a lot to do." He stubbed out his cigar in the ash-tray. He looked at her. He said: "When I was talking to Quayle months ago, when we were planning, this trip of mine to Saint Brieuc, he told me that one day they'd try to get at me. He told me that I was to give them the information they wanted, but that they had got to force it out of me; that I was to stick it as long as I could. He said they would know damned well if I talked easily I wouldn't be giving them the truth."

She got up from the table. She said: "I understand, O'Mara. Always in that peculiar service to which you and I have the honour to belong there has been an unspoken motto—'Any means are worthy for the end.' I hope the thing is as you want it."

O'Mara said: "I hope so too. So long, Tanga."

He went out of the room.

Five minutes later she heard the Typhoon as it went down the gravel drive towards the entrance.

She sat down at the top of the table. She took a cigarette from the silver box; lit it. Then she went to the door.

She called: "Yvette."

The clock on the church tower at Saint Lys struck the half-hour.

Ernestine, her arm through Guelvada's, said: "The theatre was early to-night. It was a short play—that one. It is only just half-past ten."

"I am glad," said Guelvada. "I am glad because that means I shall have more time to spend with you. I am especially glad of that to-night." His voice was sad.

"Why to-night?" she asked. She squeezed his arm.

"To-morrow I have to leave. Very early in the morning. I have received instructions. Someone is getting excited about something. I don't know what. It is all very secret."

"I am sorry," she said. "Shall you be away long, my Ernest?"

They began to cross the little square. The moon was full and the scene was delightful. The old cross-timbered houses silvered by the moonlight presented an almost unreal appearance.

"Not long," said Guelvada. "Three or four days. Then I shall return—unless, of course, they decide to send me somewhere else."

She said in a small voice: "This makes me very unhappy. Life is not good. I have been very sad about Jules. I thought that I should never recover from that shock. Then you appeared in my life, and, having wished to kill you at our first meeting, I have since found that there are many qualities about you that appeal to everything that is feminine in me. I hope that I do not sound to be immodest . . . but that is how I feel."

"My Sweet!" said Guelvada. He was thinking that it would be damned funny if O'Mara was wrong. It would be funny if he was barking up the wrong tree about Ernestine. Guelvada, whose experiences with women, in all parts of the world, had been considerable, was half inclined to believe that O'Mara *was* wrong. He thought it impossible that Ernestine should be such a good actress—*if* O'Mara was right. Especially as she *was* an actress by profession. He thought that it was so much more difficult for a woman to dissimulate about affairs of the heart when it was her business to pretend emotionally on the stage.

They passed through the narrow street on the north side of the square. They walked silently. She said nothing. It seemed that she was very sad that he was going away.

They came to the little lane that led to her house. Guelvada stumbled, fell, saved himself with his hands.

He said: "Damnation! Now I am dirty. I dislike your Saint Lys dirt."

She laughed. "Never mind, my cabbage," she said. "I have some perfumed soap that is *very* nice. You shall use it. On the way home you can sniff at your hands and remember Ernestine."

He smiled at her sideways. "I hope I shall have something better to remember you by," he said ardently.

They came to her house. She opened the door, led the way in. Guelvada closed the door behind him as she switched on the light.

He said: "Damn!" He stood in the narrow passageway, looking at the floor.

"Now what?" asked Ernestine.

Guelvada stooped, picked up a button. He said: "This is off my coat. First I fall in the dirt; then I lose a button. This is not my good day."

She said: "Stupid . . .! I will sew it on for you."

"You are a dear girl, Ernestine," said Guelvada. "I am very fond of you."

She laughed. She went into the bedroom. Guelvada opened the door of the sitting-room; went inside. He switched on the light; lit the wick under the coffee percolator. She came into the room.

She said: "Here is my own special cake of soap. Use it carefully. Whilst you are washing I will sew on the button."

"What should I do without you?" asked Guelvada. He slipped off his coat; handed it to her. He took the cake of soap; went out of the room. He squeezed her waist as he passed her.

She sat down on the arm-chair by the fireplace. She laid the coat across her lap. She looked down and saw the micro-photograph lying in the middle of the floor. She got up, put the coat across the back of the chair; picked up the photo-film. She held it up to the light; looked at it for a long time. She slipped it into the low neck of her blouse.

She went quickly to the bedroom. Almost immediately she came back into the sitting-room. She stood, her hands behind her, leaning against the wall at the end of the room—the wall facing the door.

Guelvada came into the room. He was turning down his shirt-sleeves. He was whistling softly to himself. He was smiling.

He said: "Well . . . is my coat done? Have you sewn on the button?"

She moved her hands. He saw the pistol. He looked at her. He was still smiling. He stood in the centre of the room, looking at her, smiling at her with a smile that was insolent.

He said: "Well . . . Fraulein Boche?"

She said almost breathlessly: "I am going to kill you. I am going to kill you and I shall love it. You fool . . . you thought you were so clever. You thought you were being so very clever, and . . . *look what you dropped!*"

With her left hand she took out the micro-photograph; held it so that he could see it. Guelvada shrugged his shoulders.

He said, in German: "Well . . . and what then? You are a small, fat sow, and your lips stink of garlic."

She called him an obscene name. She said in a low voice that was hoarse with rage: "You killed the man called Taudrille . . . who was my beloved husband. You thought you had been clever. Now I am going to kill you. I shall kill all of you. I have been watching and waiting my time. Now I shall watch your wriggle . . . and then the others . . . one by one. . . ."

She choked with rage. Her body shook with anger. Only the hand holding the pistol was steady.

Guelvada moved almost imperceptibly towards the sofa.

She saw the movement. She said: "Stand still, dog!"

He shrugged his shoulders again. He said: "You are mad and, as I told you before, you stink of garlic and inferior German sausage. After I kissed you I used to wash with *eau de Cologne.*"

She hissed at him vehemently: "I should like to kill you by inches. I should like to watch you die slowly, but I have no time, and I have no need of you. I know your friends . . . I know everything . . . I shall deal with them. . . ."

Guelvada looked at her with a certain pity. He said quietly: "I will tell you just what you are, you Nazi bitch."

He told her.

She mouthed something at him. She squeezed the trigger of the automatic. She fired twice. She leaned against the wall, her breath coming in thick gasps.

Guelvada fell backwards. He fell and lay still. A little froth mixed with blood came from the corner of his mouth. His eyes closed.

She put the pistol in her pocket. She moved towards the arm-chair. She picked up Guelvada's coat; began to search. She found the envelope; sat down, took out the contents; began to go through them. She read through the papers; concentrated on Quayle's note:

"The arrest of the man Liebnisch who shot and killed the woman Frayne disposes of the last of Rozanski's agents in England stop Essential both return immediately stop All arrangements made for your movement airplane Gouarec airplane twelve midnight onwards.

"P. Q."

Ernestine began to smile; then to laugh. She laughed softly to herself. She got up; stood looking at the prone figure of Guelvada. She drew back her foot. She kicked him in the face.

Then she went into the bedroom. In a cupboard in the corner was a telephone. She took it out; waited. Then, in a quiet voice, and in polite French, she asked for a number.

The antique silver clock on the mantelpiece in the dining-room at the *Villa Cote d'Azur* struck one. Tanga, who was sitting at the table, got up; walked across the room; looked at the clock. She was thinking that she had admired it when she first came to the Villa; had considered the workmanship to be exquisite. She thought that it was strange that she should be thinking about a clock at this moment.

She went to the side table; took a cigarette from the box; lit it. She wore a black coat and skirt with a frilled blouse. Her face was in repose. As she moved, her body was relaxed, her steps easy. She wondered how long one would have to wait.

She heard the click of the latch on the french windows. She did not even turn. The hand that held the cigarette was quite steady. There was another click as the french windows, concealed by their heavy curtains, were closed.

A voice said: "Turn round."

Tanga thought: Now is the time. Now you must begin to act. For some reason which she did not know she found herself trying to create a scene in her mind—a picture of O'Mara when he had first met the man Morosc, and Nago. She wondered why she was thinking about O'Mara. She turned round.

The woman Ernestine stood in front of the closed curtains. The pistol was hanging down in her right hand. Her face was pallid, her eyes narrowed. She presented a terrible picture.

Tanga said: "What do you want?" There was a small note of fear in her voice.

Ernestine said: "You. I want *you*. I have killed the other one."

Tanga said: "I don't know what you are talking about. Are you mad? You cannot break into people's houses like this at night with that ridiculous pistol." The words were brave, but her expression denoted a certain anxiety.

"It would be amusing," said Ernestine, "if I were mad. But whether I'm mad or not does not matter. You will do as I tell you."

Tanga stood in front of the side table. She said: "It is easy for you to be brave. You have a pistol. If I had it, I have no doubt I could be as brave as you."

"Why should I bandy words with you?" said Ernestine. She laughed. "You will do as I tell you. You will do as I tell you because I am your master; because I belong to the master race."

"Isn't that rather old-fashioned." Tanga smiled.

Ernestine moved round the end of the dining-table. She held up the pistol. She came close to Tanga. She raised her left hand and struck her across the face.

She said: "I have no doubt that Madame will consider that is old-fashioned too. Perhaps you do not like old-fashioned things. Perhaps you will like this better." She struck again.

Tanga said: "Have you come here to do this?"

"No," said Ernestine. She ran her tongue over dry lips. "I have come here to take you away. I have come here to get you because just at this moment you are a rather valuable person to us. There is a car outside—the car that belonged to the man you helped to kill—the man whom you thought was Taudrille—the man who was a splendid Nazi. I am glad that it is his car. I am glad that it is his car which will eventually act as a hearse for your miserable body."

Tanga stubbed out the cigarette on the table behind her.

"Go and stand over by the window," said Ernestine. "When you get there you will draw the curtains. I shall turn off the electric light. Remember that it is a moonlit night and I shall be able to see you. If you try to do anything except what I tell you I shall shoot you—not to kill; merely to disable you—and I am a very good shot. Do not think you can escape anything by trying to be clever. Now go over to the window and draw the curtains."

Tanga walked across to the french windows. She threw aside the heavy curtains. Almost simultaneously the lights went out.

The voice came from behind her: "Open the windows; turn to the right and walk along the drive; get into the car in the driving-seat. You are going to drive. I shall sit behind you. You will drive out of the big entrance, turn on to the Gourant Farm road. You will pass the farm; take the main road which by-passes Saint Lys and joins up with the Saint Lys-Gouarec road. Don't worry if you do not know the way. I will tell you. Now move!'"

Tanga stepped through the french windows. She put her hand to her face where a red weal showed.

The voice said: "Put down your hand."

They got into the car. Tanga let in the gear. The car began to move. In a minute they were on the road.

"Now," said Ernestine, "fast, my beautiful one . . . but not *too* fast."

When Taudrille's cottage came into sight, Ernestine said: "Slow down. Pass that cottage and you will find a narrow road. Turn into it, drive through the little gate on the right. You will find yourself on a piece of lawn behind the cottage. Back the car; turn it round so that it is pointing to the gate, ready to move away. Then get out."

Tanga did as she was told. When they were behind the cottage, and the car had been reversed, she got out. Ernestine prodded her with the pistol.

She said: "Through the back door there. There'll be a light inside."

Tanga opened the back door which led into the passage. She walked the length of the passage into the sitting-room in the front. The light was on and heavy frieze curtains had been drawn across the windows.

A man was sitting in a chair. He seemed to be about fifty-five years of age. He was almost entirely bald. The jaw-bones were high and protruded. The lines between the jaw-bones and his chin formed an angle. His eyes were staring and the lids drooped as if he was very tired. The hand that rested on the arm of the chair was thin. The fingers were long and delicate.

He presented a picture of repose. Except for the strange expression on his face—an expression of weariness that was almost sadistic—he might have been an old professor of languages. He looked at them with eyes from which the lustre had departed. His face was immobile.

Ernestine closed the door behind her. She stood with her back to it. She said: "Here she is. The chicken all ready for the plucking. Such a pretty chicken!"

Tanga stood in the middle of the room, her hands hanging by her sides.

Ernestine went on: "May I present Madame la Comtesse de Sarieux? This is M'sieu Rozanski. Perhaps you may have heard of him?"

Tanga said nothing.

The man said to Ernestine in a quiet voice: "It is obvious to me, Karla, that you have been letting your emotions run away with you again." His voice was dry and brittle. "I see you have already struck this woman in the face. I imagine the process was unnecessary. I have told you before that I do not like that."

There was silence for a moment; then Ernestine said in a surly voice: "I am sorry. But why shouldn't I be emotional? I am filled with hate. What do you expect me to do?"

The man said: "That is the wrong sort of hatred. Hatred which matters is always very cool and calculated. But I do not think we have a lot of time to waste. Arrange the chair for Madame. The handcuff is on the table." He smiled. "Madame la Comtesse should feel honoured. We are using the same steel handcuff for her as we used for a compatriot of hers. He was, I have no doubt, a very brave man, but eventually he did what Madame will also do. He told us what we wanted to know. The chair, Karla. . . ."

Ernestine brought the chair. She said: "Sit down. Put your hands behind you through the bars. Be quick."

Tanga obeyed. Her wrists were gripped. The handcuff went on. She was pinioned.

Rozanski produced a small silver cigarette case. He took out a Turkish cigarette; put away the case; produced a silver matchbox. He lit the cigarette.

He said: "I have examined the papers which you left for me, Karla. I congratulate you on your cycling. You reached here from the house in Saint Lys in forty minutes. You must have ridden hard. I have examined the papers. It seems we are lucky."

Ernestine said: "I am glad for you."

He handed her the envelope. He said: "I think the Movement Orders will be good enough. I don't think the passports are even necessary, but in case some fool should ask to see them I have arranged the photographs; filled in the details."

He turned to Tanga. "This is one of those occasions, Madame, when the pagan gods have been good to us. Just at a moment when I might have considered things to be not hopeless, but very inconvenient; when my remaining *agent* in England has been arrested; I find myself in a position, or almost in a position, to carry out the work myself—the work I have set myself to do for a long time, and which my inferiors have bungled."

He went on soothingly: "You will realise, Madame la Comtesse, that things have been a little difficult for us. We are a beaten nation—or at least that is what people think. Yet there are some of us who remember the great things we have done—the still greater things which we stand for. This work of mine is only a move in the game, but an important one. I have a feeling"—he smiled acidly—"that it will be successful. But we require a little assistance from you, Madame."

Tanga said: "You will get none from me."

Rozanski said: "That is a matter on which I do not agree with you. But we shall see. I do not desire to hurt people unnecessarily—not that I mind hurting them. In fact, to hurt people, if it is part of my duty, gives me a certain satisfaction—just as it might amuse me to put my foot on a rat. But you must understand that time presses. I cannot allow you any great latitude. Therefore, let us get down to business."

Ernestine said: "We are wasting time. Why should we waste words on this thing?" Her eyes gleamed evilly.

Rozanski said: "Madame la Comtesse, I am in the fortunate position of having two Military Movement Orders stamped and signed by the British Embassy, in Paris. I have also two passports issued by my Embassy in perfect order. These papers were, of course, intended for the man O'Mara, and a companion—possibly you, possibly the man Guelvada, who has been killed to-night. I require one piece of information; then the way is clear to finish my work, which ends with the death of the man Quayle."

Tanga said: "I shall tell you nothing."

He went on, as if he had not heard her: "I desire to know from you where the man Quayle may be found. It is obvious that his headquarters are moved, but they will be somewhere in London. You will tell me where they are and you will tell me the truth."

She said: "I do not know where they are. If I knew I should not tell you."

He smiled. "You are a liar, Madame," he said. "Let us see if we can refresh your memory. And you will not lie. I have always discovered that when people feel sufficient pain they tell the truth." He looked at Ernestine.

She asked: "What . . .?"

He took the plump half-smoked cigarette from his mouth. He said: "The cigarette—not too quickly; not too forcibly. I have always found the cigarette very effective with women."

Ernestine took the cigarette from his hand. She held it delicately in her fingers. She moved in front of Tanga. She stood looking down at her.

She said: "Female swine . . . talk. . . ."

Tanga said: "No!"

Ernestine put out her hand; opened Tanga's jacket; tore away the blouse from her throat. She put the lighted cigarette on the white flesh.

She said: "How do you like that, Frenchwoman?"

A little hissing sound came from Tanga's clenched teeth.

Rozanski said casually: "Stop. Give her a few seconds to think about it. Then again."

Ernestine said: "Of course. Perhaps you would like to think about it, Madame la Comtesse? The first burn is not so bad. But the second is worse. The third almost unbearable. When I come to the fourth you will, I am sure, be much more amenable."

Tanga was silent. When Ernestine had used the cigarette five times she burst into tears.

At the sixth time she talked.

Rozanski sighed. He said patronisingly: "Really a rather courageous woman." He got up slowly.

Tanga sat slumped forward in the chair. She was sobbing quietly.

Ernestine said: "What do I do with her?"

Rozanski said: "It is imperative, of course, that she dies. But it is necessary that her body should not be discovered quickly. If it were, things might still go ill with us. Someone may come to this place now that they know that Taudrille is no longer alive—the police possibly."

Ernestine said: "There is a shed outside. I think the door is unlocked. I will find out."

She went from the room; down the passageway. There was the sound of a car in the distance. Rozanski tensed. It came nearer. He heard the brakes grinding.

He switched out the light; moved quickly through the passageway. In the green space outside the back of the cottage he met Ernestine returning from the shed.

He said quietly: "Silence. Into the car quickly. Someone is here. We must get away. It is our only chance."

They got into the car. There was the noise of banging on the front door of the cottage. Ernestine let in the clutch quietly. The car moved towards the gate.

Rozanski said: "Not the main road. Turn to the right; down the lane. You can get on to the main road later. Be quick."

She did as he ordered. Once in the lane, she accelerated.

He said: "It does not matter. They will spend time on the woman."

She said: "I wanted to see her die. . . ."

Rozanski said quietly: "Karla, you have always been a fool. I have learned never to ask the impossible. We shall still succeed."

As the car swept round the long curve that ended the by-pass road round Gouarec, Ernestine accelerated. The speedometer showed sixty-six miles an hour. The long white road stretched before them, bright in the moonlight.

She said: "If only we are in time. If only we can get there before . . ."

Rozanski interrupted. He sat slumped in the passenger seat, smoking a cigarette. He said in a bored voice: "I wonder why you are so excited, Karla. And there is no need to hurry. I would like you not to drive so fast."

She said in a low voice: "Very well." She reduced speed. The speedometer needle came down to the fifty-mile mark; stayed there steadily.

Rozanski went on: "There is nothing for you to be perturbed about. I imagine that somebody has found the body of Guelvada. The Saint Lys police have been informed and they have connected the killing with the deaths of your husband and Nago. They went immediately to the cottage for some reason connected with the supposed Taudrille. . . ."

She said: "Yes . . . of course." She spoke quickly. "But when they get there . . . that woman . . . de Sarieux . . . she will tell them. They will follow us. They *must.*"

Rozanski sighed. He said shortly: "You are a fool, Karla. A moment's reflection will tell you that the police who came to the cottage will know nothing of the operations of O'Mara and his unit in these parts. Why should they? And the woman will not tell them because she will not know."

"But why not?" asked Ernestine. Her eyes were on the road ahead. She was looking for the white gates which led to the airstrip. "And even supposing she does not know . . . there is yet the chance that the pilot of the airplane which is waiting for them will know O'Mara; that he will . . ."

"No," said Rozanski. "The woman will not know, for the excellent reason that Quayle never gives any details of operations to anyone except the leader of the unit—who is O'Mara. That is common sense. It is a normal technique which I have always used myself. O'Mara will have been told, but *only* O'Mara. He, on his part, would tell de Sarieux and the man we knew to be Guelvada only what he wished them to know. That is also normal technique. You understand?"

She said doubtfully: "Yes. . . . But O'Mara. If we knew where he was. . . ."

He said with a trace of irritation: "O'Mara left this evening. He drove on to the Paris road. He will have gone to Paris. It is obvious to me that for some reason best known to himself Quayle decided to recall two of them. Either O'Mara and de Sarieux or Guelvada and de Sarieux. The decision as to which man should go was probably left to O'Mara. The fact that the Military Movement Orders were left blank indicated that O'Mara was to decide. The fact that there were also blank passports indicated that O'Mara might, in certain circumstances, have decided to go by some other route—where passports were needed—if he considered that process necessary."

She said: "Yes. I see that now. Of course you are right."

"I think that events will prove that," said Rozanski. "The fact that Guelvada told you to-night that he had orders to move confirms my theory. As to the pilot knowing O'Mara, I am sure you will find the point will not arise. If I know anything of Quayle, the pilot will receive exactly the same instructions as *I* should have given him. He would have been instructed to pick up a man and a woman who would arrive at the airstrip with the necessary Military Movement Orders. That is all."

She said: "We are there. I can see the gates."

She slowed down; swung the car through the open white wooden-barred gates that led to the airstrip.

"As you see," said Rozanski softly. "The gates are open. We are expected. All is well."

The car same to a standstill outside the lean-to shed that had served as a camouflaged control in the old days. They sat in silence.

The door of the shed opened. A man came out with a lantern. He wore a peaked cap and an old uniform with brass buttons. He came up to the car, raised the lantern, looked at them.

He said: "Good morning, Madame . . . M'sieu. . . . We have been waiting for you. Have you the permits?"

Rozanski produced the two Military Movement Orders. He handed them to Ernestine. She gave them to the man with the lamp. He examined them carefully.

Ernestine said: "If you require to see passports . . ."

"No, Madame," said the man. "I am told to expedite your journey. The plane is waiting—already warming up. Will you please take your seats. I will put the car away and tell the pilot."

"Thank you," said Ernestine.

They got out; began to walk across the grass strip. Just ahead they could see the plane.

A mechanic stood by the short flight of wooden steps against the open door of the airplane. He said: "Good morning," and yawned. The propellers of the plane were revolving slowly—the engines idling.

They got into the low-wing monoplane—an Airspeed Consul. Rozanski relaxed in one of the four passenger seats. Ernestine took the seat at his side.

They heard someone speak to the mechanic by the steps. Then the pilot got into the plane behind them. He was wearing a French flying suit, a French Air Force cap and a cheerful smile. He was young, with a neat moustache. He spoke with the accent of Touraine.

He said: "Good night, or good morning, whichever you prefer. A wonderful night for flying. I suppose you have flown before?"

"Oh, yes," said Ernestine. She gave him one of her best smiles.

"Excellent," said the pilot. "Will you fasten your belts, please? I am going to take off now."

He moved past them; pushed open the door to the pilots' compartments; squeezed through into the dark cabin. He closed the door after him; sat down in the co-pilot's seat.

O'Mara, sitting in the pilot's seat, switched on the cabin light. He looked at the co-pilot, who was smiling, his fist extended, the thumb pointing upwards.

The drone of the engines became louder. O'Mara said: "Here we go. . . ." The plane began to move along the narrow runway.

Inside the passenger cabin, Rozanski turned to Ernestine. He said: "You see . . . your fears were groundless." He stretched his long legs, settled back in his seat. He began to think about Quayle.

Now the plane was over the sea. Beneath them the moonlight shone on the calm waters. Away to the left the Saint Brieuc estuary and the twinkling lights of the cottages in the fishing village showed clearly.

O'Mara levelled off at fifteen hundred feet. Now the plane banked almost imperceptibly on a bearing slightly west of their original course. Johnny Sagers leaned across; tapped O'Mara's arm; pointed below.

O'Mara looked down. Beneath him, still farther to the west, he could see the twinkling light that might have been the masthead light of a late fishing boat.

He put his mouth to Sagers' ear. He said: "Take over . . . circle. Move when you hear the gun. Are you all set?"

Sagers said: "Yes . . . give me two minutes."

O'Mara stood up. He put his hand into the deep thigh pocket of his flying suit; brought out a .45 automatic. He took off the safety-catch. He opened the door into the passenger compartment; stepped through; closed the door. He stood, his back to the door, looking at them. He was grinning.

They looked at him. Rozanski's eyelids flickered. He did not move. Ernestine, tense and pallid, saw O'Mara's grinning face, the parachute, the Mae West, the automatic. . . .

The plane began to circle.

O'Mara set his foot against the base of the empty front passenger seat to steady himself. His voice rose above the heavy drone of the engines.

"Well . . . Rozanski . . . how do you like it?" he yelled "How do you like the idea of being delivered straight to Quayle's doorstep, free, gratis and for nothing . . . goddam you . . . how do you like it?"

He pushed past them to the rear of the plane. He stood, the automatic covering them, stooping, leaning against the side of the low fuselage.

"It's an idea, isn't it?" O'Mara went on. "But is it a good one. Maybe you'd like to be tried—like the others were at Nuremberg . . . maybe. . . . Then you'd go on living for a bit, and with a spot of luck you *might* get a word through to some of the few people who are still working for you . . . some of the half-baked fools like Taudrille, or the one who was on the Gourant road, watching me drive towards Paris this evening."

Rozanski slumped forward in his seat. His head was bowed. The woman, half-turned towards O'Mara, her face livid, began to move. The barrel of the automatic came up. She sank back into her seat, still watching O'Mara, her lips working.

"And maybe they couldn't prove anything against *you,* Rozanski," yelled O'Mara. "Not against *you.* Certainly not if de Sarieux is dead . . . damn you. They couldn't prove the things you've done . . . the things Quayle *knows* you've done. Remember some of the things you did to the last woman *agent* you got . . . the one in Provence. Remember?"

O'Mara was still grinning. But his eyes glittered with rage.

"It was foolish of you to kill old Volanon, Ernestine," said O'Mara. "Damned foolish. But you had to. You *had* to do it. It was even more foolish of you to drop that pocket Shakespeare."

O'Mara put his left hand on the emergency release lever. He said: "I'm making *myself* the judge *and* the court *and* the executioner. And pleasant dreams, Rozanski, and to you, *dear* little Ernestine . . . and to hell with both of you!"

He braced himself against the fuselage. He raised the barrel of the automatic; fired through the roof. The sound of the shot echoed through the plane.

The nose of the plane rose as Sagers trimmed the aircraft tail heavy. Then the pilots' door opened. Sagers came out; slid down the sloping body of the plane towards O'Mara.

Rozanski had not moved. Ernestine, shrieking, tried to get up. The nose of the plane rose higher. She fell back into her seat.

O'Mara threw the pistol down, pulled the emergency release, jettisoned the door, which fell away. Sagers, head first, shot out through the opening.

The plane was still climbing. In a moment O'Mara knew she would stall.

Ernestine had fallen out of her seat; lay clutching its arm . . . shrieking.

O'Mara dived head first through the opening, dropped like a stone. Beneath him lay the sea.

He pulled the parachute release-cord, dropped, checked as the parachute opened. Pictures flashed through his mind. . . . Tanga . . . Guelvada . . . .

Away on his left below him he could see Sagers' parachute, with Johnny Sagers working on the cords, regulating his descent. Below him, somewhere to the right, was the twinkling light that now flashed on and off.

O'Mara pulled the R.A.F. waterproof torch from the side breast pocket of his flying kit. Flashed it downwards. The light below stopped . . . then started again.

Then he saw the plane. It came down in a spiral dive . . . its engines roaring. It hit the sea with a solid, smashing impact.

O'Mara looked down. The sea was not far below him. He closed his eyes; waited. As he touched the water he hit the parachute harness release; disentangled himself from the parachute. The cold tang of the sea on his face was like a whip-lash.

He came to the surface; twisted the parachute harness release; lay back on the water, supported by the Mae West. On his left he could see Johnny Sagers' torch flashing. He raised his own torch; began to work the switch. In a minute he heard the chug-chug of the motor launch.

O'Mara sighed. He lay, floating, looking at the stars.

The motor boat nosed its way into the Saint Brieuc estuary. Jean Larue handed over the wheel to the Breton fisherman; came forward. He took a small bottle of brandy from his pocket; gave it to O'Mara.

O'Mara handed the bottle to Sagers. He looked at Larue. He asked: "Well?"

Larue grinned. "All is well," he said. "And the brandy is *very* good."

O'Mara said: "Tell me . . ."

Larue sat on his haunches beside O'Mara. He said: "When M'Sieu Guelvada and the woman Ernestine went into her house my people were watching. They heard the shots. She fired two bullets into Guelvada. Both through the chest . . . bad . . . but not bad enough for what she wanted. He has had a blood transfusion. The doctor at the hospital says he will get through. He is tough—that one. He . . ."

"Go on," said O'Mara. His voice was impatient.

"I was at the telephone exchange in Saint Lys," Larue continued, "as we arranged. Sure enough, she telephoned after she had found the papers. The Chief of the Rural *Brigade Mobile* and I listened in. She telephoned a house at Juan des Fleurs—not far away. A man answered, and she said something about a rose by any other name. He replied that the rose would crimson as enchantingly for him if it were not called a rose. Very pretty. This was apparently some sort of password. . . ."

"I know," said O'Mara sharply. "Continue."

"Then she said she had great news; that she must meet him immediately at the house where the man Taudrille had lived; that she would ride there at once on her bicycle; that he must be there; that he could walk it in the time. He agreed. That was all."

Sagers took another pull at the brandy bottle. He said: "Great stuff this. There's a future in it. It neutralises the wet. Have some."

He passed the bottle to O'Mara, who took it, but did not drink.

"Immediately the chief of the *Brigade Mobile,* five men and myself drove at great speed to Taudrille's cottage. The car was parked down the road behind the bushes. I went ahead and got into the loft above the front room, through the roof. There is a small trap-door in the ceiling of the front room. I opened it slightly. I prepared my pistol. I lay there and waited.

"Soon the man arrived. The tall, bald man. He came in through the back door. He sat in the chair and waited. He smoked cigarettes. It seemed a long time.

"Then the woman Ernestine arrived. She came on her bicycle. The police say that she rode like a fiend. She was in a hurry—that one. She came into the room through the back door also, and there was a lot of talk. She gave him some papers and they seemed pleased. Then she went away, out to the back."

"Go on," said O'Mara. He sat tensely, holding the brandy bottle in his right hand as if he did not know it was there.

"She went away in the car," Larue continued. "The car from the garage at the back. She went straight to the *Villa Côte d'Azur.* Henri Fernande and Louis Gaucharde—two of my best men—were stationed by the trees on the far side of the lawn. They saw her go into the room by the french windows. Soon she came out with Madame de Sarieux. They got into the car—Madame driving and the woman Ernestine in the back seat. They drove on to the Gourant Road.

"Then Fernande and Gaucharde came out of the trees on the far side and flashed a message with their torches. It was picked up by my men on the Gourant road, the switch road, the road to Gouarec, and the by-pass road to Saint Lys. Every road was covered by the *Maquis,* and every one of them could see the signal across the valley. They picked it up and passed it on. It was like the old days when the Boches were about."

Larue sighed at the memory.

"Whichever road they took we should have had them," he continued. "They by-passed Saint Lys and got on to the Gouarec road outside Saint Lys. From my place in the loft I heard the car stop behind the house. I thought to myself: Now the fun is going to start. I was ready with my pistol." He grinned. "It would not be the first time that I have killed a German through the trap in the ceiling of that cottage."

O'Mara nodded. "Then?" he asked.

"They brought her into the room and locked her in a chair with a handcuff. She would not talk so they burned her a little with a cigarette. Madame said nothing for a little while, but eventually she told them what they wanted. I did nothing, because you had told me not to act until she told them."

O'Mara nodded. "Be quick," he said.

Larue said: "I am being as quick as I know how. Then the man said that she must be killed, and Ernestine went to see if the shed was locked. They were going to put her there."

Sagers took the bottle from O'Mara's hand. He took another pull and sighed.

"I got ready," Larue went on. "The woman going away gave me a chance to flash my torch through the roof. That was the signal. Then I got ready to shoot, but it was not necessary. The police car came down the road and stopped outside. And the man got up and went out the back way. We heard them start off in the car; they drove down the lane. We did not follow them because you had ordered that."

O'Mara said: "Good . . . and Madame?"

"What do you expect?" said Larue. "Before she was married her name was de Sirac—a Breton name. Do you expect a Breton woman to be troubled by a few paltry cigarette burns from a dirty Nazi!"

O'Mara wiped the sweat from his forehead. He said to Sagers: "Give me that bottle."

He drank; threw the empty bottle into the water.

The motor boat, its engine cut, floated into the tiny basin. Larue lit a rank *caporal* cigarette. He said: "Madame sent you a message. It was somewhat strange, and I do not understand it."

O'Mara said impatiently: "It is not necessary for you to understand it. What was it?"

Larue shrugged his shoulders. "I was to tell you that she sent you her best wishes. That is the first part. Then she said that I was to tell you that she would rather be a lady who was a little burned in Saint Brieuc than a lady who was not at all burned in Rio de Janeiro. I do not know if you understand that."

O'Mara grinned. He said: "Thanks, Larue . . . for the message . . . for everything."

The Breton tied up the boat. At the end of the little quay the police car was waiting.

O'Mara said to Larue: "It was a terrible accident. One of our engines failed and we crashed."

Sagers yawned. "It was awful," he said. "I shall never forget it. I just can't think how it happened."

Larue said: "I saw it all. When we found you and M'sieu O'Mara you were both unconscious in the water. We searched for the passengers, but we could not find them. It was terrible. Also it was very lucky for you that we had this boat out so early in the morning."

O'Mara said: "Will the police stand for that?"

Larue grinned. He said: "M'sieu, you must remember that the police are Frenchmen and of Brittany. The Bretons are a very understanding people. Perhaps you will permit me to make the report."

They got out on to the quay. They began to walk towards the car.

Sagers said quietly: "It was a dam' shame about that plane. It was a nice bus. It finished the job nicely too . . . all on its own. Very good value, I call it."

CHAPTER FIVE
EULALIA

O'MARA came into the ramshackle waiting-room at the end of the main platform at the railway station at Saint Lys.

Tanga sat on the bench by the window. He thought that even against that mediocre background she made a perfect picture. She was dressed in a cherry-coloured wool travelling-frock beneath a leopard-skin coat. She wore a turban to match the frock.

She gazed thoughtfully at the sunlit countryside.

She saw O'Mara; smiled. She asked: "Have you spoken to Mr. Quayle?"

He nodded. He sat down on the bench beside her. He said: "Quayle's satisfied with everything. He sent you all sorts of nice messages. He was very pleased that Ernest Guelvada is going to be all right."

"So all is well," she said. "And what now?"

O'Mara's expression was not happy. He said: "He doesn't want me for at least six months. That is if I want to take as long as that. If I don't, he says he would like to send me back to Rio."

Her mouth tightened a little. She asked: "Then why must you look so unhappy? Before, I understood. . . . But now, why? Your bags are packed and here on the station. You have six months' leave; alternatively, you can return to Rio—if you want to do that. You would, I am sure, receive a warm welcome there. You could do all the things you want to do; you could—"

O'Mara shrugged his shoulders.

She went on, with a small note of annoyance in her voice: "Well . . . why are you unhappy? You have every reason to be glad."

He said thoughtfully: "Some things are difficult to talk of. I wanted to . . ." He stopped abruptly.

Tanga said: "Well . . . O'Mara? What was it you wanted. Or perhaps it is something you do not wish to tell me?"

O'Mara looked at the floor. He said tersely: "It is not always a matter of what one wishes."

Almost imperceptibly she moved a little closer. She said: "There are times when I do not understand you at all. You are the most definite person I have ever met. You know just what you want and how you propose to get it. Then, for some unknown reason, when you have succeeded in a difficult task, and all is well, you find yourself unhappy, without knowing why. That is not even sensible."

He said, almost irritably: "*Of course* I know why."

"So you do know why," said Tanga. She raised her eyebrows. "And you find difficulty in telling me. That must be because I am concerned. I would like to insist that you tell me about this thing that concerns *me* and makes *you* unhappy. I think that I am entitled to know that."

O'Mara shrugged his shoulders again. He took a small cigar from his case, and looked at it morosely. He said: "Very well, I'll tell you. But I'm a fool even to put it into words."

She said: "You could never be a fool, O'Mara. Tell me."

"When I was walking along the platform just now," said O'Mara, still looking at the cigar, "after I had got our tickets through to Paris and arranged about the luggage, I began to think about myself. It's not a habit I usually indulge in."

She said: "Yes? And you thought . . .?"

O'Mara said impatiently, not looking at her: "I thought that I was a damned fool. I was thinking about a villa I have near Vannes. A lovely place—the sort of place that one dreams about—the sort of place that seems like Heaven after a job like the one we've just finished." He paused.

She said softly: "I am listening, O'Mara."

"I thought," he continued, "that here I was on my way to Paris. That this evening, when we arrive there we shall say good-bye, and that will be that." He bit the end off the small cigar almost angrily. "I don't particularly want to go to Paris," he went on. "I want to go to the Villa. But I do not want to go alone. It wouldn't amuse me. There are so many things I want to talk to *you* about. So many delightful things. . . . For one stupid moment I almost decided to ask you if you would come. If, instead of changing for the Paris train, we could go on in the train we are about to take, to Vannes; take a car from there to the Villa. . . . Then after a moment I realised the idea was ridiculous."

"Yes?" said Tanga. "Why?"

"First of all I knew you would say no," said O'Mara. "Of course there was also another reason, but the second reason didn't matter because I knew you would refuse."

She said with a twitch of her lips: "I am interested in the second reason. So let us imagine that you have asked me and that I have said yes. Now . . . the second reason, please."

O'Mara said: "If you had agreed I would have been more happy that I had ever believed possible. But even so, it would have been no good. Even so . . ."

She said sharply: "I would be glad if you would not evade the issue. Why would it have been no good?"

O'Mara presented a picture almost of misery. He said: "The reason is obvious. This year . . . next year . . . sometime . . . you and I may be thrown together again on some dangerous job, as we have during the past few days. The situation might be as tough— as hard—as the one we have just experienced. You must realise, as I do, that such a thing would be impossible after a holiday at the Villa. Imagine . . . how the devil could I be prepared to take a chance on your safety; to do something as dangerous as the thing we've just completed—after we had been together? After . . ."

O'Mara stopped speaking. He lit the cigar. He got up. Stood looking out of the doorway.

Tanga in a low voice said: "O'Mara, forgive me . . . but you are a fool. And *what* a fool. You do not even realise that . . . you are so stupid that you are not even aware that . . ." Her voice trailed off into a quiet exclamation of annoyance.

O'Mara said: "Our train is in. I'll go and see about the luggage." He went off.

At two o'clock the train steamed into the junction.

O'Mara said: "We change here. Our train is at the opposite platform. I have arranged about a reserved compartment. Will you find it. I'll get the luggage transferred."

She said: "Very well. I will do that."

A porter showed her the compartment; went away. He came back in a few moments with her small travelling-bag, and O'Mara's light overcoat and gloves. The porter put the things on the seat and disappeared.

A ticket inspector came along the corridor. He looked into the compartment. He said: "Do not disturb yourself, Madame. M'sieu has produced your tickets."

Tanga said: "At what time do we arrive at Paris?"

The inspector raised his eyebrows. "This train is not for Paris, Madame," he said. "This is the Vannes train. You have just changed from the Paris train."

She said: "I see . . . thank you."

She was white with anger.

The inspector walked down the corridor. In the next coach he almost collided with O'Mara.

He said: "M'sieu . . . it is extraordinary. Madame believed that she was in the Paris train. I told her it was not so; that I had seen the tickets; that . . ."

O'Mara said in terse French: "You are the great grandchild of an imbecile. I would like nothing better than to cut you into little pieces with a knife."

The inspector said: "But, M'sieu . . .!"

O'Mara interrupted: "Listen, you ass. Take your notebook quickly and write this down. . . ." He told the man what to write; gave him some instructions. He said: "Do this well, or I will not be responsible for what happens to you." He gave the man five one-hundred franc notes.

He walked slowly along the corridor to the compartment.

Tanga looked at him. She said tensely: "I am furious with you. I dislike you *very* much. I was stupid enough to believe that you could for once be quite human; that you desired . . . that you . . ." She stopped for want of breath.

O'Mara said nothing.

She went on: "You could not risk a rebuff. You dared not take the chance of someone saying no to the supreme O'Mara. So you plotted to find out. On the station at Saint Lys you were merely acting . . . so that you could find out what I thought. So that you could find out if . . . if . . ."

She gasped a little. "And all the time," she went on, controlling her voice with difficulty, "all the time you had tickets for Vannes You had *never* taken tickets for Paris. You *knew,* but you had to be *quite* certain."

O'Mara produced a deprecating smile. He said: "A man has to take a chance sometimes. . . ."

"I desire never to see you again," she said. "I have an immense hatred for you. Your presence is unutterably distasteful to me. You . . ."

O'Mara picked up his coat and gloves. He said, unhappily:

"I knew my luck couldn't last. I'll tell them to get your luggage out. There's another train for Paris in half an hour. Good-bye, Tanga."

He went away.

She sat looking blankly at the opposite side of the compartment. She was furiously unhappy.

The inspector appeared. He said: "Madame . . . there is an urgent message for M'sieu O'Mara. It has been telegraphed from Saint Lys. It was sent to Saint Lys by telephone from the *Villa Côte d'Azur.* Perhaps you'll give it to M'sieu."

He laid the message form on the seat. He went away quickly before she could speak.

She got up. She picked up her handbag and gloves. She took up the message. Possibly from Quayle, she thought. She wondered. . . . She read the message.

It said:

"Darling stop Have been in touch London stop Told you are going Paris stop I shall be there at the Hotel Crillon stop My greetings love and devotion stop Eulalia."

Tanga stood looking at the piece of paper. A little hissing sound came from between her white teeth. She got out of the train. She walked down the platform.

O'Mara was standing by the luggage compartment.

She asked coldly: "Has my luggage been removed?"

He shook his head.

She said with a shrug: "I have been thinking that there are times when in spite of the most execrable behaviour, a man must be saved from his own stupidity, and . . . er . . ." she hesitated—"other things. I desire to talk to you, O'Mara."

He said in a humble voice: "I do not deserve such luck. . . ."

They walked down the platform towards the compartment.

She allowed the little ball of white paper to fall between the train and the permanent way.

She thought: Even the most delightful, the most courageous men are merely children.

THE END

Printed in Great Britain
by Amazon

24994034R00108